University Campus

Barnsley

The Secret to Success in the Music Industry

Hints and Tips to Help You Succeed!

Chris Grayston

The Secret to Success in the Music Industry

First Edition
Published 2016
NEW HAVEN PUBLISHING LTD
www.newhavenpublishingltd.com
newhavenpublishing@gmail.com

Cover design ©Marc White
Art ©Si Clark

newhaven
publishing

ABOUT THE AUTHOR

With over 25 years' experience in the music industry as an events director, music promoter, music manager, record label owner, distributor, song writer, producer, publisher and recording studio owner, Chris Grayston can now add author to his resume!

Chris began his career as a music promoter, organising tours and events for some of the UK's most recognised dance acts including Carl Cox, Andy C, Judge Jules, Spoony, Fabio and Grooverider. He has promoted sell-out events at Wembley Arena and The O2 in London for acts including Zane Lowe, Tinchy Stryder, Kids in Glass Houses, The Hoosiers, and Funeral for a Friend.

He moved on to developing his own record label Hectic Records which rapidly evolved into four labels. Hectic Records quickly became known as one of the biggest independent labels in the country, boasting in excess of 100 singles, over a million sales across the group and releasing over ten compilations and albums.

Over the last ten years as Managing Director for Future Music, a freelance music consultant, plus A&R scout for Sony Music, ITV, Thames Television and The Voice, Chris wanted to find new ways to reach out in an accessible way to the thousands of unsigned artists within the UK. He therefore devised national music competitions Live and Unsigned, Open Mic UK, and TeenStar in order to discover all the new up-coming, under the radar talent.

Through his constant enthusiasm and positive approach Chris has seen over 75,000 acts through these music competitions, and has been able to share his own intuitive advice to many of the aspiring passionate artists.

This new book is an insightful read into the many aspects singers first encounter when they embark on entering the music industry, and provides fundamental information to point singers in the right direction on how to make it in the industry. The book simply makes singing simple to succeed!

Table of Contents

One
SINGING AND VOCALS

BUILDING YOUR CONFIDENCE

Naturally some people have bags of confidence, but for the majority of us we have to work at developing confidence. It's important to be able to overcome stage fright, so learning to deal with the nerves is something that you need to overcome if you want to be a successful singer.

Everyone has the ability to build their confidence, and it's essential when performing and singing that you work on this before performing to an audience. Portraying confidence is an important ability for professional and successful singers.
So what can you do to build up that confidence?

Practice
It may sound obvious, but practising is an easy way to build confidence in your voice. By practising your song over and over again you will become more comfortable singing it. The more comfortable you are with the song, the more confident you'll be with performing it as a result.

It's also a good idea to practise in different settings so you become confident singing in more than one surrounding. Practise with a microphone or prop (as silly as it sounds, something like a hairbrush or bottle) and as you intend to perform to an audience on stage.

Filming your performing on your phone or camera to watch back at yourself is helpful to see how you can improve. Then consider performing dry runs in front of trusted friends or family. This will hopefully make your performance second nature and you'll know exactly what you need to do when on stage.

Learn your song

It's important to know your songs inside and out. If you are not 100% in knowing the words, phrasing and the way you wish to sing your song, under pressure this may come under strain as you will be concentrating on those aspects rather than others, such as performing to your audience and connecting to the song.

Analyse

Always watch your performance back and make adjustments to it until you are completely happy with it. Also watch YouTube videos to study how other singers including your favourite artists express emotion and perform. Hopefully you can adapt elements of their performances to perhaps use in your own. Study their mannerisms, how they use the space on stage and how they interact with the audience; this will help you incorporate important elements of performance into yours.

Singing Lessons

Working with a professional singing teacher can help you to build vocal confidence. A good vocal coach will be able to identify the strengths and weaknesses in your vocals and can help you to develop these areas. By identifying weaknesses they can find ways in which those areas of your voice can be improved.

Once you've learnt how to control the areas that aren't your strongest, you'll become more confident with your voice

Don't ever be put off by mistakes; don't let a mistake knock your confidence. If you use every mistake as a lesson you'll begin to learn what not to do with your voice and your performance. It's important to remember even professionals make mistakes from time to time; no matter how professional you are you just have to recover from them and move on.

Perform
The easiest way to build confidence with your vocals is to just enjoy the experience. When you're performing and it's clear that you're enjoying the performance, it rubs off on the audience, giving you a better reception from them. Having a responsive audience is a huge confidence booster! Try and apply it to every performance.

Remember
Practise so that your performance is rehearsed to the full and becomes so ingrained you can't forget the words or how you are going to perform. Using your phone to film yourself performing dry runs will hopefully make it clear what you will be doing when on stage and thus second nature.

Amateurs practice until they get it right; professionals practice until they can't get it wrong!

IMPORTANCE AND BENEFITS OF SINGING LESSONS

It doesn't matter if you're just starting out or you're an international singing sensation, all singers need to have singing lessons and continue with having coaching.

Find below some reasons why singing lessons can help you as a singer.

Reaching your full potential
Singing lessons help you to sing better. Although that seems obvious, that's what they aim to do. Good

14

singing tuition will help you learn techniques and exercises that are suitable for the effective development of your voice.

Staying in key

Singing consistently in key when under pressure can sometimes be a challenge due to the effect nerves can have on the vocal cords and breathing. Regular lessons will teach you how to control, manage and balance this for a successful performance.

Increasing your vocal range

Reach your potential by extending your vocal range to allow you to sing comfortably and without strain. You'll then be able to pick from a much wider range of songs and impress your audience even more.

Building confidence

Successful singers need to be confident as that confidence reflects in their performance. Confidence comes from being in control and control comes from having a good technique. Taking singing lessons can help with all of the above and will therefore enable a singer to focus less on what could go wrong and more on delivering a believable performance for their audience.

Vocal health

The voice is a very delicate and complex instrument, which unfortunately cannot be renewed if it wears out. When singing without the education provided through professional coaching, it's very easy for a singer to pick up bad habits and damage their voice, sometimes permanently.

Good singing teachers will identify where you may be putting undue strain on your voice and the correct way to change that with specific vocal exercises. They can also advise you on your lifestyle choices that could help to protect your voice.

Breath control

The health of your voice is paramount for a singer; therefore learning how to control your breath can help you to keep your voice strong. Breath control is essential to a singer, even more so when you need it to perform. If you lose your breath and stop singing, you risk ruining not only your performance, but also your reputation.

Developing your own style

Successful singers usually have something unique about their voice so that when you hear one of their songs you immediately recognise the artist. Singing lessons will help develop a strong foundation for your unique voice.

HOW TO PICK THE RIGHT SINGING TEACHER

How to choose the best singing teacher for you

Choosing the right singing teacher is such an important decision when thinking about singing lessons. Making the wrong choice in teacher can lead to wasted time, money, frustration and a loss of confidence; but worse of all, potential vocal damage. However, finding the right singing teacher can bring you amazingly fast results, confidence in your ability, an enormous amount of pleasure and even a successful career!

The right teacher should make you feel comfortable and at ease. He or she should be supportive and motivational and work with you at your own pace to bring out the best in your voice. You should not only feel and hear improvement in your voice but you also really enjoy the experience.

Below are some pointers to think about when choosing the right singing teacher.

Recommendation
If you already know of singers with good voices find out who they take lessons with. Do some research on your local teachers; good references and recommendations are always a good place to start.

Websites
The best way to access everything you would need to know about your potential singing teacher is if they have a professional and up to date website. Looking out for information on the techniques they teach, relevant training, styles they teach and testimonials should all help you to be able to determine if they're going to be a good choice for you.

Are they qualified?
Qualifications are not always essential, but they can be a good guide to help you decide which teacher is best for you. Don't be too quick to base your decision on whether they have a degree, a multitude of letters after their name or whether they have had a dazzling and successful singing career themselves.

Having the discipline to study and pass exams does not automatically equate to being an effective and inspirational singing teacher, and being a great singer often doesn't translate into being a great teacher or coach! It is however an essential requirement that a singing teacher can actually sing as they will need to use their voice to demonstrate a multitude of examples of singing exercises to you.

Lesson format

It is crucial that the teacher you choose is prepared and able to devote a good proportion of the lesson time to teaching you vocal technique. This should be done through the use of exercises that are tailored specifically to your voice type. A quick warm up will not be sufficient to develop the technique you will need to enable you to sing a song competently from start to finish, and omitting this important stage could ultimately cause vocal damage.

Do their students sing well?

This best gauge of a good teacher is to be able to hear the results their students have achieved as a result of having lessons with them. Obviously if they have dramatically improved it is a massive indicator that they are a good singing teacher.

Their voices should sound individual and stand out for the right reasons, so avoid working with a singing teacher whose students all have similar issues with their voices such as: nasal, strained, shouty, breathy or overly stylised, to name a few.

Although recommendations are a great starting point for you to find a teacher, what is great for one person is not always going to be the case for you. Make sure you are given the opportunity and time to ask any further questions you may have.

Singing style
Probably just as important as any of the above tips, don't forget to pick a teacher appropriate to the music you want to sing. If you want to be a pop singer then avoid a teacher that is classically trained, otherwise you may just develop a classical twang that will take considerable time and practice to unlearn.

Try and test
A good teacher will be more than happy to discuss lessons prior to you making a booking. Most singing teachers will be more than happy to offer a "taster" or special introductory lesson which is a perfect opportunity for you to make your choice.

Once you've made a decision ask the teacher (if they don't already) to record the sessions and review them on a regular basis, around every three months. See your improvement singing the same or similar songs and be prepared to change singing teachers if you don't feel you are progressing.

Whatever you do, practise in the "right way" daily and train with a qualified teacher on a regular basis; if funds permit ideally at least once a week.

PROTECTING YOUR VOCALS AS A SINGER

The importance of caring for your vocal cords

For a singer the voice and vocal cords are the most important part of their body. Like a footballer's legs, without protected vocal cords a singer cannot perform. When you're tired or unwell, it's important to know how to care for your voice. It's also just as important to know how to warm up correctly before performing in front of your audience to not damage your vocal cords!

What if I'm feeling unwell but still considering singing?

When feeling unwell, always keep your fluid levels up by drinking plenty of water. Taking cough medicine to stop excessive coughing will help to stop any further damage. Boosting vitamin C levels reduces inflammation and sitting with your head over a bowl of steam eases congestion and provides hydration to the vocal cords.

Vocal warm ups

If it is necessary to perform whilst you're still feeling unwell, make sure you do a longer warm up than usual to help prevent further damage. Warming up before any show is essential. Just as you are likely to pull a muscle without warming up before exercise, the same is true with your vocal cords and putting extra strain on your vocal cords without a warm up can cause permanent damage.

To warm up your vocal cords make sure you are in good posture, release any tension in your jaw and make sure you breathe deeply. Do some scales and tongue trills to relax your tongue.

Do not ever try to sing if it hurts or feels difficult in any way and seek medical advice.

Lifestyle can affect your voice
You should try to avoid speaking and shouting loudly where necessary. This causes the vocal cords to squeeze together, creating trauma. The same happens when you whisper.

Keep your vocals hydrated. Drinking two litres of water a day is what is recommended. Within two hours before performing it's important to drink plenty of fluid to lubricate the vocal cords. Keep the fluids at room temperature if possible; icy cold water or boiling hot tea aren't what you want to be dousing your vocal cords with.

Don't smoke
Smoking is an absolute no no for singers! Try to also avoid dairy products, citrus fruits/juice, fizzy drinks, coffee or alcohol especially on or before the day of a performance. Anything with caffeine in it will dehydrate the vocal cords.

Avoid stress and stay relaxed especially as you're leading up to a performance. Make sure you also get plenty of sleep!

Try and keep your physical health in check, especially if you intend to perform and use the stage. Being fit will help you to avoid becoming too breathless which may affect your singing when performing.

Eating well with a balanced and healthy diet will also help you to keep fit and strong so don't underestimate its importance.

HOW TO WARM UP AND PREPARE YOUR VOCALS

Warming up your voice fully is important as it protects your vocal cords and prepares your voice to perform at its best! A warmed up voice stands out in comparison to one that's not.

Good posture
Having the correct posture when warming up helps with the airflow through your body. The best way to stand is with your legs shoulder width apart and your feet firmly on the floor. If you choose to sit rather than stand, sit on the edge of the chair, back straight, and don't lean on the chair.

Deep breaths
Most people have the poor habit of using only the top of their lungs; make sure you avoid this. If you feel tense at all whilst breathing it will show through your voice. Keep your shoulders low and your chest relaxed.

No hot or cold drinks
Room temperature water is the best drink to warm up your voice with. Avoid dairy drinks such as milk and milkshakes completely as they coat your throat and don't let all of the voice through. Hot and cold drinks have negative effects on your vocals before a performance.

Ease all tension and relax your body

This will ease your mind and steady your voice. Try having a small snack to settle your stomach, but not so you feel full. A banana is a good example. Chewing gum can help relieve tension in your jaw, but if you haven't eaten, don't chew for too long as it can cause digestion issues.

Release your jaw

Relaxing your jaw allows for the best movement when singing. It's best to massage your cheeks with the heel of each hand and exercise your jaw by opening and closing your mouth.

Do scales

Practising scales will help you to see what you're comfortable with and what may be a struggle on the day. It also prepares your voice for every note you're likely to hit during your performance. Gradually build up your scales as starting too high or too low will damage your vocals.

Hum

Humming helps to cool down your voice, but also helps to warm it up without the straining of singing. Humming through the scales is an effective technique to ensure your voice is warmed up before performing and to protect your vocals.

Make a "mmm" sound in your own spoken voice like you're agreeing with something or have just had something tasty to eat. You should feel a gentle vibration in your throat and on your lips. Once you've mastered it and it feels really comfortable try to hum through various scales. Perhaps then try broken up notes, 1 per note "mm, mm, mm," and also in 1 long "mmmmmmm" smoothly across the notes.

Failing to warm up your voice correctly risks not only a poor performance, but also damaging your voice in the long run. You should never sing at full volume without fully warming up first.

SINGING DYNAMICS

Varying dynamics whilst singing

You must never underestimate the importance of using various vocal dynamics to enhance your performance. Dynamics are a tool that all singers can use to bring a performance alive, convey emotion and prevent their performance from being static.

There are many ways to incorporate dynamics into your performance, from simple things such as increasing volume and varied harmonies to changing phrases and delivery. Below are just a few ways in which you can use vocal dynamics to improve your performance.

Increase or decrease volume

This is a dynamic singers can use to help the emotion from the song come across during their performance. Many singers choose to increase the volume in their vocals when they hit the most emotional part of the song, but also consider decreasing the volume at certain points as it emphasises the parts where you increase the volume. The key here is to vary your volume throughout the song.

Articulate through characterisation

If you're singing a happy part of the song, try to reflect that in your vocals. Although it may not necessarily fit with the song as a whole, it will give an extra dynamic to your performance.

Change vowel shape

It can often be difficult to find ways to make your song stand out. Changing vowel shape can be a subtle way to do this. A good example is pronouncing 'me' as 'may' in an appropriate song; this can subtly add something unique to the performance.

Add silence/rests

Of course during your performance you want to be singing for most of it, but sometimes adding silences or rests makes the following vocals sound more impressive and adds more drama to the performance.

Phrasing

Extending a phrase rather than keeping it short and taking a breath can often provide a new dynamic to the performance and can help to show off your vocals.

It's not necessary to try to use all of these vocal dynamics in one performance; if you try to use all of them you risk the performance sounding too messy. However, it's important to develop the use of dynamics throughout your performance. Singing the verse and the chorus in the same way throughout the song is just going to become repetitive, so you must look to add some dynamics to avoid the performance being just a loop of the first verse and chorus, which can become quite dull and boring.

It's important to remember that not all of these dynamics will be suitable for every singer's style of vocal. It's wise to know which ones suit your vocals and which ones don't work for your vocal.

SINGING WITH EMOTION

The power of emotion is very important when singing

During a vocal performance, one of the most important jobs a singer has is to express the emotion of the lyrics and the song in their performance. Learning how to embrace the power of emotion is vital for giving your audience a convincing performance and conveying the lyrical content. In order to do this you must connect to the song and then connect to us as an audience.

Many artists will experiment with different vocal qualities and changes in tone in order to learn to add emotion or edge to the lyrics. The tone of our voice generally carries much more meaning than the words we actually say, so practising methods to vary vocal tone is a sure fire way to improve your overall emotive performance.

Ways you can change vocal quality and tone

Your vocal tone is determined by a few important factors, one of which is the position of your larynx. The larynx is the grouping of muscle, cartilage, and ligaments in your throat, commonly referred to as the 'voice box'. Making use of the different positions of your larynx will allow you to produce different vocal tones and sounds, which if used correctly can help you add more emotion to your vocals. Experiment with this and if this doesn't come naturally it's something you could work at with your vocal coach.

EMOTIONAL CONNECTION TO A PERFORMANCE

Connecting emotionally to an audience

Although your singing ability is important, performing songs in an engaging manner is even more so. The main way to win the hearts of your audience is to inspire an emotional connection to the song you are performing. Singers need to bring life to the emotion in the song and connect the audience to these emotions. Singing with feeling is essential and portraying the correct emotions of the song in your performance is critical.

Creating an Emotional Connection

Making an emotional connection is paramount for singers because it will change your creative process for the better. You need to reach out to the audience and connect with them.

Learning how to embrace the power of emotion is vital for giving your audience a convincing performance and conveying the lyrical content successfully.

For some creating an emotional connection will come naturally, for others it will take time to develop. The more you perform, practise and analyse your performances the better you will become at expressing emotion.

Song choice

Song choice is immensely important to singers, so first things first make sure you choose a song that you can relate to as well as sing. When you can relate yourself to a song, you can easily get into the right character for the song. Capture the emotions, feel them and express them through your sound and performance. Before you start, make sure you understand the lyrics and sing them like you're telling your story. Whatever direction you take, be sure to make the song your own. This is your performance not a copy of another artist's.

To reiterate, song choice is everything so choose a song you care about. Caring about the meaning behind the song you are singing improves your performance as connecting with it adds more real emotion.

Singing dynamics

Using appropriate vocal techniques and singing dynamics will help you build an emotional connection with the audience. In particular by varying the volume and tone of your voice in your performance, you can draw people in and lock in their attention. Different feelings have different sounds and tones.

Facial expressions

Facial expressions are a great way to help communicate inward emotions to your audience. Communicating emotion with your facial expressions will enhance the particular mood of the song, which will also add dynamics and further help the audience connect with your performance.

It is important that your facial expression matches the feeling of the song. It's no good having a frown on your face if the song is upbeat. If your expressions aren't matching the feeling of the song your audience will not connect to it.

The most common cause of not matching facial expressions to songs is by not focusing on the words or timing. A good way to combat this is to practise your song in front of a mirror and/or film yourself to find an expression that looks genuine. Eye contact is also really important to connect with your audience. It's also worth considering acting or drama lessons to help build your stage presence and learn to act out the emotion.

Body language

Body language is just as important as the ability to sing. Imagine watching a musician singing on stage and they just stared at their feet as they sung without moving; it would be a horrific performance. Body language is a further tool in which you can convey the song to the audience. Always remember when singing on stage, body language is important but it has to be fitting to the performance: don't move just for the sake of it!

Audience engagement

Engaging with the audience is essential when performing on stage. It can be from simply smiling and giving eye contact to show that you're enjoying yourself, or using facial expressions to reflect the emotions of the song.

It's not all about the voice when performing; you need to be able to create audience engagement so they are able to connect and relate to you. If you are performing a song where you can't make use of the stage as easily, it's even more important that you don't forget hand gestures and facial expressions which can help to enhance a performance. It is important to have a presence on stage which lets the audience know that you are confident in your singing abilities.

If you choose the right song, it will help you to create audience engagement. If you can connect with the song emotionally you are more likely to sing from the heart, making you feel more confident and believable to the audience.

31

DICTION FOR SINGERS

What is diction?

Diction is the style in which you pronounce words or sounds.

The importance of diction for a singer

Clear diction is very important when singing for a number of reasons, so it should be focused on when developing your voice. The two main areas to consider when working on diction are performance and technique.

Make the lyrics clear

From a performance point of view, when singing a song you are, in most cases, telling a story or sharing thoughts with your audience. Therefore it's vital that you can distinguish the lyrics in order for your listener to understand what the song is about and what the message is. If the lyrics to a song aren't clear, then the song becomes meaningless and forgettable and you will lose the audience.

Diction technique

From the technique side, for some singers words can be slurred, mumbled and very lazy sounding. The most common causes of this can be all of or any of the following: mouth shape, tongue placement, external muscles around the jaw or internally in the larynx, breathing or style choice.

Always record your performances and if you continue to have issues with diction then a good vocal coach should be able to assist in resolving any issues.

Improving the clarity

Working on improving the clarity of vowels and consonants and therefore the enunciation of syllables can have a major impact on how easy singing can be. A great tip is to relate back to how you speak, so you stay truer to your own voice. When you talk you seldom squeeze or strain your vocal cords or become overly slurred and breathy. This is because you're using your voice in a way that is most natural to you without trying to manipulate muscles to search for certain notes or add a vocal style that takes your voice way out of balance.

If you have a tendency to rush and mumble your speech you will find by working on your diction for singing that your speech will also improve.

Vocals coaches for diction

There are elements of diction that can be worked on with vocal coaches by using appropriate exercises that will undo bad habits and start building new ones with correct technique. Although this may feel difficult at first, with practice you'll be surprised how quickly the new techniques become second nature to you. You'll find the tone, clarity, range and control also improves as a result of clearer diction.

If you are working with a vocal coach, do make sure you're clear on the style of singing that is right for you. Good diction is important across all styles. However for some styles, it is much crisper, for example Classical and Musical Theatre, whereas in other genres you can get away with less crisp and pronounced diction.

Two
PERFORMING

IMPORTANCE OF SONG CHOICE

Why picking the right song is so important
Picking the correct song can define a singer and maximize their chance to shine. Here are the important things to take into account when making the decision!

Firstly make sure the song suits your vocal style and range. Selecting a song that really shows off the sweeter tone in your range is always going to show you off at your best. Working with a vocal coach can really help you establish what this is, or just keep recording yourself and evaluate. It's pointless selecting a song that is going to be a challenge to sound good at either low or high notes, especially when performing and when the vocal is under pressure.

Know your voice
Knowing your voice is important so that you can access your strengths and weaknesses to ensure you know what to develop. With this knowledge it then makes it easier to know what key and range of song choice is best and what key to write songs in.

Pick a song that you can make your own, but only if it's not too farfetched. Amongst the considerations are that it needs to be appropriate to fit your image, style and age.

Don't pick popular songs; there are millions of songs to pick from not just the current most popular choices. No one wants to hear the same song repeated numerous times especially at an audition. In general avoid this as unless it's vastly different to the original it's going to be difficult to stand out.

Is it best to pick a song to show off my vocal?
NO!! This is a really common error and is a poor reason for a song choice. Selecting a song just on the merits of showing off your vocal is such a common error. Don't take on an epic, powerful song by someone like Whitney Houston or Adele as this is a huge risk and can only result in leaving a bad impression of your talent. In a pressured environment if it doesn't sound as good as the original, people will criticise it.

Far better an idea is to pick a song that you like that will help you connect with the emotion in the song, but don't pick a song just because you like it. It needs to showcase your singing abilities and your unique artistry, so if that means picking a song you don't normally listen to, then that's what it has to be.

A lesser point is pick something modern, or if you choose an old song put a modern twist on it; also select a song that is applicable to your age. Being different and making it you own is far more important.

You need a song that, if performed in front of an audience, will resonate with them so they can connect with you and the song.

Use the resources at your fingertips
If in doubt, ask for feedback from a vocal coach or trusted friends and family. Perform the song for them, ask for their honest opinions and ask open questions. At the end of the day song choice is down to you, the singer, but constructive criticism can help you realise if the song is working.

You may read this repeated on a number of occasions throughout the book and I'm not going to make an apology as it's the core to development: recording and/or filming a demo of you performing the vocal to a backing track can also help you hear your performance. You and others can analyse it and see if there are any changes you can make to make the song work.

And remember song choice isn't everything; just as important is the consideration that you will also need to perform, add dynamics, engage with the audience, connect to the music and bring out the emotion of the song, otherwise the performance will be lifeless and all the hard work selecting the song choice will be partially let down.

It's a lot to remember so that's why it's important to focus on the basics which all comes down to doing the hours of practice!

AUDITIONS TIPS

Pointers on how to impress

Be Prepared
Firstly, if you've put yourself forward for an audition, you must be prepared for anything that may happen. Know your song inside out; don't ever read the lyrics off a piece of paper as that shows you have not practised and are not ready. You should practise so much that you can't get it wrong.

Check your gear
If using a backing track on a CD make sure it works correctly on a number of formats and also take a backup on a different format like a memory stick. Avoid having a backup on your phone as it will have to rely on the connection. Double check the track is the right song, and ideally the only song to minimise the risk of errors.

If you're playing an instrument, have it tuned already and have spare parts with you, such as fully charged batteries, spare strings and a strap, all of which you will need at some point for the day when they decide to break or stop functioning. Also a tuner is handy even if you normally tune by ear, just to double check the tuning.

Look the part
You have to impress both visually and vocally, so having the right outfit can affect your audition. Your outfit needs to reflect who you are as a person and what you're singing; so select outfits that stand out, you feel comfortable in, reflect your personality and the music you are performing. Many acts have carved a reputation for what they wear over and above their music at times.

Be original
If you're auditioning for a record or management deal they are most likely to want to find something new that they don't already have, so make sure your performance is original and memorable. If you've got an original song, then play it: it shows courage.

Try to relax
Easier said than done but if you've built the confidence you must learn to live with the nerves and don't let them control you. Always remember those judging you will want you to do well! So you've obviously potentially got something they want. Keep composed and take a few breaths so you don't rush the song.

Perform

It's not just about singing, you've got to be able to take that song and make it a performance. You have to own the stage, make the audience believe it's yours. The most successful artists can make the whole crowd believe in their performance.

Communicate

Understand what you're singing, know what the message is behind the song and let us know through your performance. Eye contact is a strong way to communicate with your audience and make sure the expression shows through.

Listen

Auditions are a great way to receive feedback and it is likely to take many auditions before you start to have success. So try where possible to get feedback for your audition: it might be the constructive criticism you need to make that next step. Make sure you look at your feedback, as you might not be aware of the one thing holding you back.

Enjoy yourself

Music is a beautiful thing and as singers you all have a common passion for music. Make sure your audience know how much you're enjoying the performance and that this is all you want to do.

SOUND TESTING

How sound testing works and how to get the best

This is about the difference between being happy or not with your sound during a performance. Sound testing is the time to decide on your levels, correct any microphone technique, listen to yourself through the monitors and mentally warm up.

Arrive on time for your sound testing

First things first: a sound engineer and/or stage manager is not going to be impressed if someone uses up their precious little time by running in late. Avoid scrambling around for your instrument case and tuning up on stage. Make sure you turn up on time and ready for your sound test.

You never get a second chance to make a first impression, so be early and introduce yourself politely to the sound engineer and/or stage manager during the sound testing when appropriate and maybe offer to buy him/her a drink (optional). If the offer of a drink is not accepted just tell them where you will be and inform them you will be ready when they are, selecting a place out of their way but in their eye line.

Be prepared

As well as being on time for your sound testing, make sure you are tuned up if you have an instrument or have completed a vocal warm up at least. Ahead of the day make sure all your equipment is reliable, works and you have spare batteries, straps and leads if applicable. Be ready for a quick switchover between acts and you'll look good if you're prepared.

Be honest

The whole point of sound testing is to correctly set up the levels in the venue and that includes the (fold back) monitors that you will be hearing during the performance. Be honest with the engineers if you'd like your vocals louder or your guitar with an EQ boost. Consider the sound in the venue will always be different empty and with an audience. Always make requests in a polite manner!

Don't hold back

As mentioned before, the idea of sound testing for singers is to set up levels, so if you're holding back and not playing or singing as loud as you would do in the actual performance, it becomes pointless to a degree. A lot of venues have digital desks so they can automatically store your settings. It doesn't make sense to store it all and then have the sound engineer re-adjust when you come out hitting notes twice as loud as the first time.

THE PERFORMANCE

Performance advice

Performing is one of the most important parts of being a singer; it is the element that takes an act from being just a singer to an artist. Being able to perform on stage is a skill that all singers should master if they wish to be successful in the music industry. Here are a few pointers on how to perform well on stage.

Use the space

Whether you are on stage or in an audition room use the space around you to perform. This doesn't necessarily mean you have to walk over every inch of the stage, but make use of it, don't let the space swamp you. Have your spatial awareness about you. As long as you are confident in your abilities, entertaining should come naturally.

Whether you are using a lead or wireless mic and/or a stand or not, you can still move around more at the upbeat parts or even use your arms to highlight emotional parts of the song. Getting close to the front of the stage helps to engage and connect to the audience too.

Facial expressions

Facial expressions are really important when you are performing. Not only do they help you convey the emotion of the song to your audience, but they also help to connect with your audience. If you're singing a sad, emotional song, bring that pain or sorrow into your facial expressions and if it's an upbeat happy song be sure to have bright and fun faces.

What is also important to remember is to smile. Even if you are singing a sad song there are always appropriate parts to come out of character which allow you to smile. Smiling shows you are enjoying yourself, which makes the audience enjoy the performance too. Eye contact is also really important to connect with your audience.

Convey emotion

During a vocal performance, one of the most important jobs a singer has is to do is inject emotion into the lyrics of the song. Learning how to embrace the power of emotion is vital for giving your audience a convincing performance and conveying the lyrical content. Many artists will add different vocal qualities and changes in tone in order to add emotion or edge to lyrics.

The tone of our voice generally carries much more meaning than the words we actually say, so practising methods to vary vocal tone is a sure way to improve your overall performance.

Look happy to be there and interact with them during and after songs. Showing them that you are having fun.

Body language

Your body language gives the audience an idea of how you're feeling when you're on stage and conveys the emotion of the song. Making eye contact with the audience helps them to connect with you; it shows you're confident and again adds to the interpretation of the song.

Standing tall and having good posture not only helps your performance, it makes you look professional. Body language is a main tool in expressing the emotion of the song so making sure your movement reflects this is key. It will take time to perfect but it is essential to start incorporating it into your performance.

Know what to do with your hands! If you are flapping them about or have them in your pockets it's not going to look that professional.

Always remember when singing on stage, body language is important but it has to be fitting to the performance; don't move just because you feel you have to.

Steal moves from the big guys

Take some pointers from well-known singers. Don't copy one person, and don't copy large parts of their routine, just adapt little bits from here and there. Look at YouTube videos of artists you are influenced by and watch how they perform with their mannerisms and look at how they convey emotion in their performance. It may just be an act, but that's what you aspire to be.

Take stage tips that you feel you can accommodate in your personality as an act and appropriate to the emotions of the song. Take the bits that you enjoy the most and make them your own.

To Stand or to Sit?
Both standing and sitting on the stage have their benefits. Sitting is well used in a more intimate setting, perhaps during open mic events; however, be aware that you will have to compensate for not moving with facial expressions, hand gestures and eye contact. Standing gives you the freedom to move wherever you like and is a more open style of performing. You can of course incorporate doing a bit of both.

Keep your hands busy. It is a common mistake for singers to just hold their hands by their sides or in their pockets where they are least effective. Some techniques to implement could include clenching your fists, swapping the microphone between hands and moving the microphone stand.

Think about image

Having your own image that reflects your personality is important, but what is more so is matching your performance and song choices with your image. It's essential that what you perform musically matches your image and style. You also want to be comfortable with what you're wearing during your performance.

You could consider bringing in a gimmick. Costumes are a common one, wearing something that will get people talking, or creating some stage props to have on hand to mess with. Only use it if it can be maintained. If you get too hot, you can't take the costume off mid set. It needs to be something achievable.

ON THE DAY

Performance tips for on the day
Being a good stage performer is something that will set your performance out from the rest. It's not only about how to sing the song; it's also about how you perform the song! Appropriate to some performances, it's important to be pragmatic and be able to adapt to the situation so consider the following to give you the edge on the day.

Keep an eye on the atmosphere
Bear in mind the stage and venue size. What would have seemed atmospheric on a little stage may not work on a larger stage. During shows try and look at how other acts are performing on stage; watching a variety of acts you can see the atmosphere amongst the audience and how it can change rapidly.

Analyse the performances of others singing during sound check or by watching their performance. Think about the best spots to walk to and from, or where to place yourself for your dramatic final note. Notice how and where the lighting is set up on stage and avoid areas where it is dark.

Make an impression from beginning to end
Walk confidently on stage and maintain that confidence throughout your performance. It's easy to tell which performers are nervous when they walk on stage and it often takes a while to fade. Even

established acts get nervous but learn to act to hide the nerves. The more performing you do, the easier this should get, even if the nerves don't go.

Another good way to make an impression when you enter the stage is with your image. This is dealt with in more detail in a later chapter.

If you've not been announced, announce yourself when you come on stage but no more. Thank the audience at the end of your performance, and let them know you're grateful they watched you and just quickly where they can find you.

Be confident
The key to being a good stage performer starts with confidence. Performing live can be a daunting task. There are lots of things happening such as feeling a mixture of emotions, including nervousness and excitement.

Try to remain unfazed as over the course of time you may encounter technical glitches and bright lights making it hard to see amongst lots of other problems that come with a live performance. They will initially be a challenge to you first time round and will throw you from how you have normally practised.

Movement
Being a good stage performer is about moving around on stage. If you can master the act of grooving to your tunes, you will go down a lot better with the audience. Make sure it is appropriate though. The whole idea of being a good stage

performer is for it to be fitting and come across as natural.

Communication
Being a good stage performer is also about communicating well with other act members and the audience. Looking at random audience members in the eyes and singing along with your other act members all adds to a rounded performance.

This will help you forget about the nerves beforehand and people will recognise that you're creating good stage presence.

Engage with the audience
Engaging with the audience is very important when performing. It can be from simply smiling and giving eye contact to showing you're enjoying yourself to using facial expressions to reflect the emotions of the song. If you have a song where you can't make use of the stage as easily, don't forget hand gestures can help to enhance a performance by reaching out to the audience.

Make use of props and dancers
Make use of whatever you have to work with. You've got a stage so move around it. You've got a mic stand, so use it during the softer bits and take the mic out when the song becomes more upbeat. Don't be restricted by your props.

Dancing whilst singing
If you've got a really upbeat song, why not bring some dancers along? Not only will it be a more enjoyable performance but also a more memorable

one. Of course you are only as good as your worst dancer, and ensure you get involved in the routine so you are part of the performance. Plenty of practice is essential! If you go down this route you will also have to consider your fitness. Doing large parts of the routine could affect your breathing and vocal control in general.

Never stop
Whatever mistake you make when performing, never stop and/or apologise, you will only highlight the mistake! Chances are the audience didn't even notice it. Most importantly avoid long pauses.

You will always make mistakes, so just give a little smile and the audience will hopefully warm to you if they are aware you have made a mistake; this will come across as professional, confident and charming.

Always record videos of your own performance
You can then review it back and see it from the audience's point of view, which may be uncomfortable to begin with but is also critical in seeing how to improve.

PERFORMING WITH MUSICIANS

As a singer your only instrument is your vocals, which you will want to accentuate as much as possible. That is why it is really important that when you are performing or recording music that you work with good musicians who are going to accompany your vocal at least at the same level and highlight your voice to its best potential.

You must always remember that you are only as good as your musician.
Performing with a musician who plays out of tune or who is inconsistent with timing is only going to reflect on you and in most cases put you out of tune or mess up your timing.

Further you could find and perform with the best musician in the world but they also need to be as committed as you, so they need to be always on time, motivated to practise and willing to do gigs and performances at the drop of a hat, otherwise you will always be chasing them and it will become draining and tiresome.

You must have synergy
This is important on a number of levels. Firstly if the musician is part of your act on stage then it is important that there is a synergy of image i.e. they look part of your act. Secondly there should be a synergy in the performance, that they do perform and they feel part of the act. On stage it is important visually to have an engagement and understanding between singer and musician.

The above will all come together if you practise hard, communicate well and have the ability.

Show a connection on stage
There is nothing worse than seeing two or more performers not connecting: it just feels like you are watching solo performances and that one or more of

them doesn't want to be there. This falls back to the same disciplines we keep mentioning; keep practising, analysing and practise some more!

What makes a good musician

A "good" musician doesn't just mean that they are technically advanced or experienced on their instrument; obviously that is important, but it also refers to your compatibility with them. As a singer you need your accompanying musicians or band to work around you. If you make a mistake a good musician should be able to improvise around it making the mistake appear intentional.

Communication between singers and other musicians is also really important. Singers need to be able to indicate when the musicians need to slow down, speed up or stop the music, often through signals that can be integrated into their performance so that the audience are unaware of their directions.

Building relationships can often take a long time, but working with good musicians is essential to giving the best performance you can.

DEALING WITH NERVES

Tips and hints on dealing with nerves before you hit the stage

Most if not all people have to deal with nerves before heading on stage and they are perfectly natural. Dealing with nerves can make you feel shaky and nauseous and can cause a lack of focus and concentration. Nerves are normal and help focus a performance so the key is to control your nerves and to not let them take over you.

Learn to live with the nerves
You need to learn to live with the nerves and embrace them as in reality they will never go, you just must learn to live with them.

On the day, the aim is to try and ease all tension and relax your body. This will ease your mind and steady your voice.

Watch what you eat and drink
Try having a small snack to settle your stomach, but not so you feel full. A banana is a good example. Chewing gum can help relieve tension in your jaw, but if you haven't eaten, don't chew for too long as it can cause digestion issues.

Avoid caffeine as it can enhance anxiety. Instead try drinking herbal tea or some lukewarm water. Ice cold or boiling hot water can shock your vocal cords and make them close up.

Dealing with nerves

The best way to deal with nerves is to be confident in the first place. Having practised and performed so many times that it's second nature will reduce the amount of things that can go wrong. As always perform to friends, at open mic nights, film yourself, ask for feedback first and analyse. Visualise your performance and go through it step by step. Begin by thinking about heading down from the dressing room and following it through to going on stage and hitting those first notes.

Show up early! This will relieve any nerves about being late or having any last minute hitches.

Call a friend

Who better to assist in dealing with nerves than your friends and family? It can help to talk over your issues and normalise and rationalise them. Laugh often! It helps with dealing with nerves in more ways than one. A hearty laugh fires up and cools down the body's stress response. In a similar way to exercise, laughter can cause a temporary increased heart rate and blood pressure, which can lead to a state of relaxation and help deal with nerves.

Consider whatever works best for you, so consider watching a comedy film in the morning or hanging around with friends before the show. Put yourself in a place where laughing will relax you and ease the nervousness.

Exercise
Ahead of a gig in the evening try and get some exercise! Aim for at least half an hour. From a jog or a long walk to a weight lifting session, this will all release tension and get the endorphins going.

Walk away nervous energy
If nervous at the gig, walking around even for just ten minutes can help in dealing with nerves. Studies have shown that walking can help spark nerve sensors in the brain to relax the senses, so taking a walk even an hour before the event can help you feel more at ease.

Meditate
Try meditating. It may sound silly, but it can help put you at ease. Mediation is not for all but for some people it can play a big part in dealing with nerves although it takes some practice. Find yourself a quiet spot, preferably away from other people, and sit or lie in a comfortable position and shut your eyes. Think of anything that relaxes you, anything that isn't your performance.

Close your eyes or focus your gaze on the floor and concentrate on your breathing. Feel the air fill your lungs and inhale and exhale to the count of three. Whilst in meditation mode, it's important to let thoughts pass through your mind without judgement. Remember, we are working on dealing with nerves here, so try not to distract yourself with unnecessary thoughts.

Listen to music.
Listening to music can also help deal with nerves; classical and jazz music have especially been proven to lower heart rate, blood pressure and stress hormone levels.

Try creating a pre-show ritual. You would be surprised how many singers have one! Whether it's something as simple as having a game of pool two hours before the show or something more complex like an hour gym session followed by a walk and ending up with watching your favourite TV show, if it works for you and puts you at ease, do it!

WHY IS EYE CONTACT IMPORTANT?

We've touched on this already but eye contact is so important when you are performing to an audience. Not only does eye contact help you convey the emotion of the song to the audience, but it also helps the audience connect to you as a performer. As we know performing is one of the most important parts of being a singer, so knowing how to entertain your audience through your performance and facial expressions is crucial. Eye contact is an essential ingredient to this.

Watch other performers' performances and see how they engage with eye contact.

The importance of eye contact

As a performer you need to be able to connect to your audience and create engagement with your audience so they're on your side. It is important to have a certain presence on stage, which lets the audience know that you are confident in your singing abilities. What you do with your eyes during a performance should be determined by what is artistically appropriate to the song or performance. You need to avoid looking at the ground and actually engage with your audience through eye contact, giving the audience a reason to keep their eyes on you. You'll make the audience feel special if you communicate strongly through eye contact, as if you are performing the song just for them.

Overcoming the fear of eye contact

Avoiding eye contact with the audience due to stage fright or shyness is not uncommon, especially for novice performers; the problem with this is that the audience will feel a similar discomfort if you never look at them. Appropriate eye contact can give you greater command of your stage presence.

As difficult as it may seem to overcome the impulse to not look at the audience, if you don't you may always appear to be a novice. A way to overcome this issue is to look at a point just above the audience if you are performing in a big room or at an audience member's head, as they will think you are looking at them. Gradually you will be able to become confident enough to actually look in their eyes.

Using eye contact appropriately

If you're singing a sad song, closing your eyes may be the best way to convey the mood, so don't be afraid to do this if it is appropriate. There are many situations however when looking directly at your audience is exactly what is needed to create the most impact emotionally. If you look them straight in the eye it can make your performance more powerful and really engage your audience. Let your song interpretation dictate what you do with your eyes.

TIPS ON BEING IN A DUO OR GROUP

How to be successful as a singing duo or a group

Many singers choose to sing and perform with other people rather than going solo. Ensure if going down this route you make it for the right reason.

The problem many duos and groups face is that they all have something individually, but often struggle to make it work together in a group.

It's important to remember that a duo or a group is only as good as their worst performer. It might seem an easier way of performing as there are more people in the group to share the roles, but it doesn't always work out that way. The most successful groups play on the strengths of each individual and try to highlight those whilst performing.

You don't all have to sound the same

Many groups struggle because they fail to layer up their harmonies and instead make all the harmonies the same. Without layering the vocals you risk sounding like a solo act or by being slightly out of time can end up sounding like a car crash. When performing it's important that the vocals layer up well to show off how diverse the act can be and what they're capable of.

Dynamics

In relation to the above point on harmonies, it is even more important to ensure as a duo or group you work the dynamics individually to work collectively.

Interact and engage with one another

Just because individuals within a group have their own role doesn't mean that there can't be interaction within the group. Interaction and engagement with each other can show chemistry and unification. This is all part of an act's image. You want fans to feel that you are fun and want to be part of the group. It's often difficult for groups to interact with each other as they're too focused on what they have to do. To avoid this it's best to work out how to interact with each other when rehearsing for your performance.

Image

For a group of singers there is a stronger need for the image to be worked on because you need to look like an act, not a group of individuals. The art of synchronisation is something all duos and groups should master to look more like a group. Having a strong image, as with any act, is even more important with a group to express an identity that can help to develop the act as a brand.

Routines

Being in a duo or a group you should bank on having to work twice as hard to get it flawless, especially in terms of a performance. Just singing won't be enough. A good way of enhancing a performance within a duo or a group is by incorporating a routine into a performance. This keeps the audience watching and shows the group are more than just individuals singing, they are a group that can sing and perform.

Get it right and it can work with powerful effect, get it slightly wrong and it can come across as very amateurish. As always the key is practice and preparation make perfect.

Three
USING THE TOOLS

MICROPHONE TECHNIQUE

How your microphone technique can improve your performance

(Credit to Julie Miles of Vocal Ovation for additions): Mic technique is often overlooked as one of the skills you need to become a successful singer and performer. However, the way you use the microphone can affect your performance in many ways.

Get comfortable with the microphone

When first starting out it's only natural for singers to be very nervous when given a microphone for the first time and it often comes across in their performance. Feeling tense and holding a mic awkwardly can really affect your vocals more than you would imagine, so get to know the feeling as early as possible by practising.

If you don't own a microphone then use a prop; although it may seem a bit lame using a bottle or hairbrush, it will definitely get you used to that feeling and soon that mic will be just like an extension of your arm and, more importantly, your voice!

Sing into the microphone

Make sure you sing right into it. It's one of the simplest techniques but it's so SO important. Singing directly into the microphone allows all of your vocals to be fully projected. Most microphones have a radius around them that will detect noise, it's important to hit this radius with every note you sing.

Sing with the microphone too far away from your mouth and you won't allow the tones, dynamics and power of your vocal to be fully captured. Already you could be at a disadvantage to other performers on stage who have mastered their technique. Ideally you should keep the mic one or two centimetres from your mouth at all times except for the high or more powerful notes.

If you turn and move round the stage always maintain the same distance and if you use it as part of your performance during instrumental breaks always make sure you bring it back to your mouth. If you don't the projection of your vocal will be inconsistent and you'll lose key elements in the performance of your song.

Sing into the microphone how you would usually sing

This may sound really obvious but this is especially vital for that all important sound check as the sound engineer will set your levels based on the vocal volume he or she hears. If that changes dramatically or is inconsistent in either the sound check or the actual performance they'll simply have to guess when to put your vocal level up and down. Whether you manage to get away with it or not, chances are it will result in you not sounding your best.

Avoiding feedback and distortion

Feedback is that awful sound the microphone gives out that causes everyone to wince a little. One of the most common ways for a microphone to affect your performance is with feedback from the speakers or monitors. Take time to check where they're situated on the stage and simply avoid getting too close.

Distortion occurs for a couple of reasons, one of them being a singer holding the microphone too close or too far from their mouth. The distance from your mouth to the microphone is essential as it can make your vocals sounds muffled and distant. The other reason a singer might notice distortion is when the volume is too high on their microphone. Keep the volume low enough to allow you head room to project and not peak which creates distortion.

Balance on the volume control

A very common problem singers face during a performance is not getting the balance right between the backing track and the microphone. You want the backing track to be loud enough that you can hear it but also so you can hear yourself. This can vary a lot depending on the quality and production of the track.

If you don't have a sound engineer, the best way to solve this is through trying out various settings until you're happy. Ideally have a third party present standing near the back of the room where you'll be performing to ensure the microphone is loud enough for you to be heard but not be overpowering.

High notes

Hopefully you will have practised your song to give dynamics to the performance and emphasise the low and high notes. This is the time you will need to pull the microphone away from your mouth on the high notes or risk feedback and being too loud – how far you pull away really depends on the volume and power you sing them with.

Far too often this is ill timed by singers and they pull the mic away too quickly thus losing the projection where it's needed at its most for impact. Timing is crucial and observing other seasoned singers as we've mentioned before, on YouTube for example, can really assist you to nail this.

Microphone tricks

Having strong microphone technique can really help a singer enhance their performance. Breath control in particular when holding a note is crucial. If you have little breath left by the end of that important sustained note, a sudden dip in power is going to be very noticeable to you and your audience. Try pulling the microphone away from you then bring it back as the note ends. It should sound as if you held it consistently and the audience will be left remembering the power you still had to the very last second – very impressive!

GUITAR PLAYING TIPS

Guitar playing tips to help you when performing with a guitar

Suddenly with a guitar in hand it can throw off even the most experienced of performers, so you will need to think of yourself as starting performing from scratch. You will need to build your confidence and perfect your stagecraft. So the disciplines are very much the same as we've covered before.

Rehearse your set like you would play it live. That means ad-libbing in between tracks and thinking of some small talk, which is better than the average 'give me a second...' whilst you tune up leaving the audience in silence.

Film yourself

Filming yourself is always a good idea and may help you pick out your own faults before you get to the stage of performing to the public. For example, if you notice that you close your eyes too often or your right arm is particularly stiff, you can alter these before your important performances. Often performers find that they are looking down whilst performing with a guitar; this is a habit that cuts off engagement with the audience. Filming yourself is one of our most effective playing tips, as it's a performance angle that you'd not normally see.

Play low stress performances
Performing with a guitar can be a daunting situation so it's a good idea to try out some methods of performance with friends and family beforehand. Set up a microphone stand as you would have in a stage setting and try out different methods of performing with a guitar. This gives you access to honest criticism from your select audience and can help refine your act.

Also consider some local open mic nights. That way it's not going to be so crucial if you mess up and again if you film it you can constantly review and refine.

Make sure your guitar is set up
It's important when performing with your guitar for your instrument to be in tune, your strap to be the correct height, and your batteries to be new if applicable. Also remember to carry back up equipment like spare batteries, cables, strap and picks; there will be one occasion you will need it so be prepared.

Consider buying yourself a pair of strap locks to protect your prized possession. It happens too often that a guitar strap doesn't fit correctly or is weak and it breaks on stage.

Play with enthusiasm

The audience doesn't necessarily support the most talented performers, but rather the most enthusiastic ones. Extra points if you're both. Enthusiasm doesn't have to be loud - sincere love of what you're playing is enough. Enthusiasm is contagious, and truly enthusiastic performances are generally rare and appreciated. Be one of these performers!

HOW TO USE DYNAMICS WHEN PLAYING GUITAR

You don't have to be an expert guitar player to add dynamics to your performance. Start with what you know and experiment with guitar dynamics from there!

Using different dynamics is essential when playing guitar as dynamics help to spice up your performance, and also your song writing. Using dynamics can help you to make your performance stand out from the crowd. Dynamics are a simple way to add emotion and expression to a song when playing guitar.

Go from hard driving section to a soft section

When playing the guitar it can be easy to fall into the trap of playing the same riff you've become comfortable with since you started playing. The problem with this is that your fans are unlikely to stay interacted with your music if all of your music has a familiar sound.

Therefore using guitar dynamics exercises you can help to build the melody in different ways for each song you compose. A popular technique is to contrast between hard driving sections to a softer section as it allows the song to breathe.

Change the intensity

Changing between picking and strumming when playing guitar can be the easiest way to work on your guitar dynamics. The benefits of picking the guitar are that you get a more mellow sound from the instrument, whereas when you're strumming it can help to build up a livelier section of the song. You can consider striking a balance between both intensities using guitar dynamics.

Put silence/rests at the end of a section

Using silences and rests in your melody whilst playing the guitar can add extra dynamics, which helps to bring more emphasis to specific areas of your song. Silences and rests can be used to emphasise a lyric, or even just to build anticipation for the next section of the song.

Change the tempo

Another way to bring dynamics to your performance when playing the guitar is to change up the tempo of the song to spark the attention of the listener. The tempo of the song is the speed at which the underlying beat goes, and altering this can be an interesting way to bring dynamics to a song when playing the guitar.

A slower tempo will help give a mellow feel to the song, whereas a faster tempo gives an upbeat impression. Changing up the tempo can help to bring more of an effect to the song and helps the guitar player to emphasise certain sections of a song accordingly.

Volume pedal
A volume pedal can be used to vary the volume of a performance and create wild dynamics. Volume pedals are popular as they are easier to use than the guitar's volume control, mainly because they can be operated hands-free, making it easier to do more complex tricks. Using a volume pedal for playing guitar can help to regulate the volume of the instrument and ensure solos and rhythm sections are all played at the same level.

Whatever you do keep it simple; there is no substitute for a good song and performance. These dynamics should aid that so don't get too carried away.

PERFORMING WITH MUSIC KEYBOARDS

How to perform with music keyboards and sing at the same time
Normally when preparing for a performance most people only have to worry about their voice. But by including an instrument, such as music keyboards, you have to put double the amount of work in to make sure your performance is remembered for the right reasons, and not because you started playing the wrong keys.

Preparing for your performance

Whatever you do make sure you are stage ready to perform with music keyboards and sing. The temptation is to start performing on stage too early and spend most of the time looking down at the keyboard - this is not performing!

Using your space whilst performing with music keyboards

Just because you may be rooted to one particular space on the stage does not mean you can't engage the audience and get them on your side. What will really set you apart from other performers is the way you can still communicate your message through eye contact and facial expressions, and really commit to the performance, regardless of keyboards between you and the audience.

As always you will need to express the emotion in the song so if appropriate don't be afraid to kick your chair back and stand up. The more passion you give and the more you enjoy it the better the performance. If you have to keep looking down during your performance, and have nothing but a blank expression on your face, then perhaps you are not stage ready.

Always remember that there are huge resources at your fingertips. Study other performers' live performances on YouTube or your favourite artist at a concert. Start to pick up what works and what doesn't for various performances. Then try and test them out yourself.

Get the right posture

It's very important when performing with music keyboards that you have the right posture. Whether you decide to sit or stand, you should retain a flexible feeling in your spine. If you do slump, your breathing and control of breathing will be affected, which will essentially impact your vocals. To stop this try not to lean forward - your ribcage should stay in its rightful position and not collapse forward.

Do keep in mind that you don't want to be too rigid, as this will look unprofessional. Just because you have music keyboards in front of you doesn't mean you cannot still get into the song and enjoy yourself. If anything the movements you make are even more crucial as they are limited. You want the audience to be on your side, and not feeling disconnected just because there's an instrument between you.

Getting the mic right

Making sure your mic is in the right position is paramount to making sure you keep the right posture. You want to make sure the mic is close enough to your mouth so you don't have to lean, and high enough to make sure your spine stays tall, but not covering your face so the audience can't see you expressing the song.

Keeping power in your vocal whilst performing with music keyboards

Just because you are playing music keyboards doesn't mean your vocals should suffer. If you choose to sit when playing the keyboard, a good way to maintain power is to sit on the edge of your seat and squeeze your bum against the seat. This way you will get as much power to your voice as if you were standing.

Don't go too early
You must remember that your voice takes priority and playing music keyboards should be secondary. If you're not 100% confident in playing the piano then you need to keep practising before hitting that stage. If you can't play without having to think about the next key then this can lead to poor performance, so make sure you're completely ready before performing on stage.

Four
WRITING SONGS

WHY IS IT SO IMPORTANT?

On a very basic level as a singer you are only likely to make money when you perform. As a singer songwriter you open up so many potential opportunities and avenues.

Open doors
As a singer unless you sing original material certain doors and places to play won't be available to you. Many open mic nights and festivals will only want artists that play their own songs, so by performing your original songs you will make these opportunities available to you.

Record labels
Record labels as a general rule are looking for acts that are songwriters, as they know that's where the money is; otherwise you need to demonstrate something quite unique in your talent and personality to be signed. If they do sign you without you writing your own songs it's just another thing the label needs to develop.

Money
The money in music has in recent times been in the writing of songs. Regardless of who is performing the song, or where and when, you should receive money each time it is played. This can be quite significant, so if you have a successful song but you played no part in the writing of the original song for the band

or group you are in you are unlikely to receive a penny.

Songs can get you signed

There have been some massive notable examples of acts who wrote for other artists that had huge success from the songs and as a result the songwriter has received a lot of attention and a spotlight to launch their own career.

There are no guarantees that just because you can sing and perform that you are going to be a songwriter too, but the thing to remember is that just like your singing, just like your performance, it needs to start from somewhere! Eventually even if song writing doesn't come naturally you can at least get to the level of being a co-writer and as a result you will receive credit and a cut of the money.

HOW TO WRITE SONGS

Be creative and emotional when song writing

Writing songs and song lyrics is a lot easier if you focus on something you are interested in and passionate about. Think of relating your lyrics to what's happening in your life or how you're feeling about a certain situation. One way is to perhaps channel your emotions into a chosen topic that is really close or important to you. You will find the whole process a lot easier.

Get creative

Song writing is something anyone can achieve if they put their mind to it, but it's important to understand writing song lyrics takes a lot of discipline and dedication. Just because you are a good singer or performer doesn't mean to say you will be a natural songwriter but by working at it you will develop the skills.

Get personal

Writing song lyrics is a very personal process; every songwriter will have a different style and approach. Use bad, funny, ironic and/or life experiences to your advantage! These are the type of songs fans can relate to. Many popular songs are about heartbreak and failed relationships.

If you convey emotion in the song people are far more likely to relate to it, if it's an emotionally motivated song. If it's a fun song, make sure it is fun and engaging and has strong hooks to leave people humming and the song stuck in the listener's head.

If you're stuck wording your idea, jot down notes of what you're trying to get across. Come back to it later with a fresh mind

Don't get stuck and share the love.
Don't waste time on a small part of your song. If the words aren't coming naturally then they probably aren't right for the song.

For some people writing song lyrics can be daunting, so try writing with someone else. Sometimes song writing works better if there's someone else you bounce ideas around with! You might find that someone who can play an instrument can really help especially with melodies, leaving you to concentrate on the lyrics, which generally comes more naturally for singers who haven't played an instrument.

What's most important
The first time your fans hear your song they will only hear the parts that stand out the most. This is why it's important to have a lyrical hook in your song! If you don't have potential hooks to your song it's not going to appeal to anyone.

The first line is very important to get right. This line introduces the song and establishes the song's mood. It's the line that grabs the listener's attention so make the most of it!

Not every line needs to rhyme. Sometimes this sounds forced and hard to relate to. Don't shy from ending lines with the same vowel sound as this is far more subtle than forced rhyming. An example could be using 'home' and 'room'.

Song structure

Make sure when you're writing song lyrics that the song has a clear structure and progression. This is particularly important if writing lyrics portraying a story. Always check your song makes sense when you read back over it.

There are no rules but a typical song structure you could try would be having four verses, each with four lines, plus a four line chorus every two verses. You could also try putting in a middle section, known as a 'bridge'.

Use the tools

Again use the tools at your disposal. Download lyrics from the Internet, to look at the breakdown and structure of songs you'd like to write like and analyse. As with all this development there are NO shortcuts and so doing the research/training, whatever you want to call it, takes as long as it takes. You cannot cheat the learning process.

WRITING LYRICS – GETTING STARTED

The basics of writing lyrics

Writing lyrics is something anyone can achieve if they put their mind to it, but it's important to understand that writing lyrics takes a lot of discipline and dedication. Writing lyrics is a very personal process; everyone will have a different style and approach but here are some basic principles to help write efficiently.

Tips for writing lyrics

There is no right or wrong way of doing it but in general you will find it much easier writing lyrics if you sort the melody first. Every songwriter's process is different, but more often than not the melody will come more naturally than the lyrics!

If melody is not your strong point then look to work with a musician, someone who can play guitar and/or piano to assist you. Searching or listing online is a good way to source like-minded songwriters to work with.

Once the melody is down, get writing! Write whatever comes into your head and don't edit your thoughts. Write down any of your thoughts or record yourself talking over the melody.

Song writing life hack

Alternatively and a good exercise when starting out is to try writing lyrics of other artist's songs in a different way by selecting your favourite songs and downloading the lyrics. Try and come up with different lyrics for every line.

It's good practice and will help you develop your song writing skills. It will particularly help with structure and ensuring the lyrics scan across the melody, a really good fun way into writing lyrics. This also doubles up as a great way to do a creative cover or come up with a track that is completely different if it develops to be original.

Write until no more words pop into your head. Once the basics are down, you can start tweaking the words you have written. Even if they don't make sense at first, eventually the right lyrics will jump off the page.

Writing lyrics – be patient

There is no right or wrong when it comes to writing lyrics but it's likely everyone will suffer from songwriter's block at some point! Don't worry, be patient! You can never force it so be patient and wait for inspiration.

Don't expect immediate results. It will potentially take lots of goes until everything gels; perhaps hundreds and hundreds so don't be too critical of your work to begin with.

Don't be afraid to leave a song if you're not feeling it - great songs take chemistry and sometimes the hook and essence of the song can come together in minutes. Other times songs take days and days, so there's no need to force it, know when to let it go and just start a new song.

Five
YOUR BRAND

PICKING A STAGE NAME

A stage name is worth consideration
You don't have to, but if you have a common name or one that is difficult to spell or remember then maybe it's worth considering a stage name. A stage name could really aid recognition.

Another consideration is online searchability. If there is a person with the same or similar name as you who is already famous it's ideal to tweak it to be unique; otherwise the previous person who was famous before you will come up first, unless you really make the big time.

Picking a stage name is something that needs a lot of thought, simply because that will be your brand once you've become successful. It should be unique and stand out. So here are some ways to help you pick one.

Avoid obscenities
A stage names is your professional name, and the name you'll be known as in the industry, so it's important to ensure that your name can't be linked with anything that may cause offence to anyone.

Choose a persona
You can't be more than one person, so make sure when deciding which name will match a narrowed down persona. Keep it simple yet effective. It is also

important to make sure your image reflects your stage name; without synchronisation you'll lose your identity as a singer.

Pick a unique name

Picking a name that no one has is a difficult task to complete, but there are ways around it. Emeli Sande chose to call herself Emeli rather than her actual name Adele because Adele was already a successful brand name. Having an individual name means that once someone has heard that they will know exactly who is being spoken about.

Other inspirations for picking a name include for example: Lady Gaga was inspired by her favourite song by Queen being Radio Gaga and Katy Perry used her Mother's maiden name (Kathryn Hudson).

Keep it simple

Ideally you'll choose a stage name that's easy to pronounce and even easier to remember. You're more likely to become a household name if people can remember your name as an artist.

Register your name

Once you've been through the process of selecting a stage name, make sure no other singer is using it and thereafter you can then register the name. This way whilst you're becoming successful no one else can use that name to make money.

FINDING AN IMAGE

Tips on creating a brand for yourself

This is one of trickiest things to get right as an act. Your image is your brand and it's one of the things the public are likely to remember about you and what will make you stand out even before they have heard you. It is likely it will take many attempts before you settle on an image that truly represents you and your music.

Have your own style

The reason many singers have done so well is because they've created their own style and used it to their advantage. It's not always about being the sexiest or best looking act in the industry although that can help; it's about having a style that reflects your personality and stands out. Lady Gaga and Paloma Faith are perfect examples of artists that have input their personality into their style. It's important that what you perform musically matches your image. The most important thing to remember is to be comfortable on stage with what you're wearing, if you know it's likely to eat away at your confidence.

Look at other artists with similar music to you and see what image they've adopted. YouTube and artist websites are a great resource to observe what others are doing.

Consistency is key

Your image is the thing that sells you when you're not singing. Therefore making sure you are consistent with all aspects of your brand is essential, from the logos on your artwork and your social media to your outfits and promotional material. You want the public to recognise your brand instantly; if they click on your website or your Facebook page it should be obvious they're on the right page and that this is the act they saw perform that night.

Get yourself out there

The best way to find your image is to physically go out, perform and see what you're comfortable with. Playing at regular gigs will give you a sense of what you're comfortable wearing and what songs you get a good response from. This experience will help you to develop yourself as an artist.

Don't define yourself by a genre

Be hesitant about your music being labelled as one specific genre as it will restrict your image. You're still trying to find what's best for you as an artist, so restricting your image to one genre can potentially hold you back and not allow you to express all areas of your personality within your music.

No apologies in repeating this: do the research, constantly look at other artists on the Internet and observe what they do.

ACT IMAGE AND SYNCHRONISATION

The importance of making your image recognisable

As an act you have to have the whole package; right down to your style choices and social media artwork it needs to be uniform and consistent. Your image and music is core to you being successful as an act and they must therefore reflect your personality and music along with hopefully standing out. Find some tips that will help you with image and synchronisation but be aware this isn't an evening or two's work - it could even take years and will constantly keep evolving.

Image

Your image is a way to market yourself when you're not performing, so considering all factors of your image is vital. Ensure your style reflects your music and matches your fans' perception of what they expect your image to be. It's also important to think about which instruments you choose to use when performing - use what suits your performance, not what you want to be seen using.

Of course if you have backing musicians and/or singers you must make sure they are well considered and that they also fit with the overall image plan.

Coming up with an image and style will take time and a good way find ideas is to look at acts with similar musical tastes. Along with your own style and personality start to incorporate ideas that you are comfortable with on stage. Again the Internet and YouTube is a huge, easily accessible resource right at your fingertips.

Social media
Social media is an essential tool for a singer, therefore making sure there's some synchronisation in all of your social media platforms is important. Try not to confuse your fans by making each one of your social media platforms different. Make sure your Facebook cover photo is the same as your Twitter header, and your SoundCloud display picture is the same as your website display picture. Make sure it's as uniform and consistent as it can be.

The amount of times I've looked at an act's social media and considered whether it's actually the same act I've watched that evening or the day before - it's essential it's all the same!

The same goes for your URL's; the more synchronised they are, the easier it is to find you. We live in an instant age and if you're difficult to find online people will be distracted and move on, thus losing you a potential fan who could have come to the next gig or shared your music to their friends. This uniformity also strengthens the brand.

For example Open Mic UK use similar URLs to increase searchability so that they are easy to find. It may not always be possible to get all platforms the same but spending time to get this right from the start will be a huge benefit:
- www.twitter.com/openmicuk
- www.facebook.com/openmicuk
- www.openmicuk.co.uk

Promo
Promoting yourself is an important part of being a singer, so make sure your posters and leaflets are synchronised. Making them look too varied, as mentioned, can only give room for confusion. If you have a running theme within your artwork it's easier for everyone and also saves you spending money on different artwork. So make sure the same logo, text font, layout and picture are on your flyers, posters and your merchandise.

Genre
The best way to become an artist that has many fans is to not label yourself as a particular genre; this can sometimes alienate certain fans. By not labelling yourself you're open to play anywhere that is credible. After you've played a few gigs you'll start to realise and get a feel for who your fan base is, then you can start pin-pointing them.

Whatever you do with your image just be yourself and love what you do as passion will shine through.

WORKING ON YOUR BRAND

Developing your brand as a singer

Your brand is the thing that sells and defines you when you're not singing. It's the image you reflect to your audience that helps them to decide whether you're for them or not. Having a positive and strong brand is important, as it'll be what people think of when someone mentions your act. Below are some tips on how to develop and strengthen your brand as a singer.

Positioning yourself in the market

Branding yourself as an act is ultimately about positioning yourself in the market. There are ways to go about this, for example how you dress may be a way to position yourself. The best way to work on positioning yourself is to find successful artists similar to your sound and see how their brand works for them. Perhaps there is something you can share or adapt in their image.

Making your brand consistent

Being consistent throughout your brand is essential. There's no point in developing your brand if you're going to chop and change it every five minutes. There has to be consistency between your image, your artwork, your merchandise etc. For the sake of your brand and for your fans, consistency saves potential confusion between who they're watching perform and who they're looking at online.

Synchronise your social media

Again, it's really important that you use the same display pictures, backgrounds, names and colour themes throughout all your social media pages! Using the same imagery across all your promotion and social media sites strengthens your brand as an artist. It looks more professional and official. People won't wonder if they are on the correct page if everything matches as opposed to having different themes and pictures on each account.

Make your brand memorable

Your brand has to be something you're remembered for. It should be unique and an extension of your personality; if it's different people will remember it and it will stand out from the crowd so don't miss this opportunity.

Your look isn't enough

Of course, the first thing people will judge you on is what you look like as an act, but that may not be the lasting impression they have when they leave. Lots of acts are remembered or liked for reasons other than their voice and their look. For example, some fans might like Bob Geldof simply because of his political views and some might like acts due to their stance on issues like the environment. It's all about the brand and the whole package of an act, not just the image and voice.

Once you've got it flaunt it

Fans love to see what their favourite artists are up to, so make sure you upload new pictures and videos regularly. The more you engage with them on a personal level, the more they'll engage with you. And as always make sure posts are interesting and/or engaging.

Six

WHAT YOU WANT THE WORLD TO SEE

WEBSITES

The importance of an effective website for singers

An effective website is essential for any act as it is the one place totally under your control that can host all your music, photos and videos together. It's the one place you have full control of the content, layout and design whereas all other social platforms decide what and how people see the platform, so essentially you have that control.

All your social media platforms and activity should link into drawing your audience to your website and therefore directing them towards the website.

Why does a singer need their own website when they can use Facebook or Twitter for free?

Because promotion is all about professionalism! Record labels and promoters want to see if you are the real deal. Anyone can make a Facebook page, but a personal website will show your dedication to becoming a success.

This doesn't mean social media platforms aren't more than useful tools, but a singer's website is where they can be represented concisely with a range of pictures, videos, news and music all clearly labelled and easily navigated.

You need a website

The underlying, paramount principle when promoting yourself is that everything needs to drive traffic to your website. Not your social media platforms. They should be engaging people to click on the link to your actual website. It's the only place that people can get a clear snapshot of what you do in a way you want to present it. So websites should include where to see you live, where to buy your music/merchandise and get a different vibe of what you are about; music can be visual too.

Every promotional post from Facebook or Twitter and every gig you promote should have a link back to your website. The purpose of these social media platforms is so people can find you and go to your website to find out more! History tells us that social media platforms dictate to us how we can communicate on their platform, constantly changing, sometimes overnight, potentially meaning losing easy communication to hundreds and thousands of the fans you've built up - you might suddenly have to learn how to reach them in different ways or in most cases pay to reach them.

Your website means people are visiting a site dedicated to your act.

WEBSITE CONTENT AND DESIGN

How to make the most of your website

Go and surf pages in general on the Internet and you'll notice that your subconscious will decide whether you like that page within about ten seconds.

So the importance of making it easy on the eye and engaging to the user is essential. In some cases it may mean you have about ten seconds to keep people on your website before they click off, carry on surfing the Internet and forget about you.

How to use your website effectively

Firstly you need a clean and clear website that features the best of what you do always - quality over quantity! Keep themes and display pictures the same and make sure those chosen are the ones used on your social media. If necessary, change the pictures on your social media so they are consistent and in line with the website, thus keeping uniformity at all times.

This comes down to image but you don't want a potential fan to question whether that is you so make sure image is the same across the board.

Make sure your website is...?

It is essential that your website is easy to navigate for all users and this includes pages being quick to load. Often hosting large files such as videos and pictures will slow down your page speed. It's best practice to host videos on another platform and with regards images, you can easily resize any images appropriate to a website to ensure it doesn't slow down your page speed.

Data capture

Data capture is very important for keeping fans up-to-date with newsletters so consider adding an option to join the mailing list on your site. Make it easily accessible and clear at the top of the website and keep it simple - a two-step process, enter your name and email address, click submit- done.

Data capture of emails is a great way to build a mailing list! Just ensure you then manage it by communicating in a regular and informative manner.

Website content

A useful idea for your website is to have updated information populated from your social networks, so include social media plugins as they will keep the content updated with fresh news and information. It also reduces the need to constantly add content to your website.

By including plugins for social media sites on your website it keeps the website updated automatically when you update your social media sites like Facebook events/pictures or a Tweet. This is a very useful way to manage content when under time constraints, as well as ensuring all bases are covered uniformly.

Lots of links

Make sure you're directing fans to the correct part of your website. People want to buy your music and/or see you live so make it easy on the eye and easy to find. If posting about your new single, put the link to the area that the fans can buy it from e.g. www.mywebsite.com/buy-single-here. If advertising an upcoming gig, make sure interested fans are directed to <u>www.mywebsite.com/buy-tickets-here</u>.

Synergy of your website and social media

We talked to death about making sure your profile pictures on all your social media including Facebook and Twitter are the same as the main picture used on your website to create a working synergy across all of your platforms. Make sure your social media sites have the URL of the website as prominently displayed as possible. For YouTube you may have to include the full web address if you include the http://.

The same applies to colour themes and logos; you want to make sure that your style and imagery is demonstrated clearly to increase brand awareness. This all follows on to physical marketing and promotion.

SOCIAL MEDIA

Building a fan base online

It's best when starting out as a singer to consider the need to build a fan base to follow you as early as possible. Your fan base will hopefully be the people to support your gigs and releases and without them you will struggle to go far.

How to build your fan base from the ground up

Key to building a fan base as a singer is gigs, events and social media. The emergence of social media in some respects makes it a lot easier to reach out but the difficulty is with keeping a fan base engaged and connected. Here are some pointers on social media and how to go about building a fan base from the ground up.

Make sure your act is sorted! Really think through whether you have the right sound, the right image and any recorded material is up to scratch. You have to be the complete package worth promoting. Promoting and marketing is so much easier when the product is good.

Create the accounts

Create your social media accounts. Facebook and Twitter are the essentials. If you are uploading video content consider creating a YouTube account so you can have your own channel on there. Ensure all themes, display pictures and such are synchronised across all platforms. You need to be sure people will look at each profile and know they are on your official page.

Create your own website. This is where you want to direct online traffic to from your social media pages. This will be your main hub and centre of activity. This should have everything about your act and should be accessible to the public. It should contain information such as: a biography, photo galleries, videos, contact information, an option to sign up to a mailing list etc.

Personal blog
You could consider writing blogs as this can gain you interest and attention. Sites such as Tumblr or WordPress allow you to do this. Write about your personal experiences or give tips you have picked up to try and help out other singers/musicians. People will read it and take an interest in you. Ensure you link back to your website.

Know how to use social media properly
The most important thing when building a fan base is to know how to use each different social media platform properly.

Facebook: Aside of your website this for many acts can be the hub of all major activity, just because so many people have accounts and use it on a regular basis. It is where news gets posted, where gig dates are announced and the longer, more important stories are posted.

Twitter: This is where you post updates on smaller activities; for example, something funny that has just happened or what instrument is being recorded in the studio as you type. Twitter is about more frequent, smaller stories than Facebook.

YouTube: YouTube is one of the most interactive ways of promoting yourself. Videos of yourself can easily get spread around the Internet and you can gain fans from all across the world not just your area.

Instagram: This is for sharing snapshots of what's happening in your world visually. Share things such as the new EP artwork reveal, latest photo shoot and gig pictures. This is where they are best off being posted.

Tumblr: Tumblr is mainly used for blog writing. This is the site where readers will want to read the longer, more informative posts as opposed to short statements.

Be warned though; avoid spamming your social media. Fans dislike spam and it could have a negative impact on your following. If fans get annoyed with your posts, they will un-follow you. Keep it professional and don't post the same thing over and over.

You must engage
Make sure you connect with your fans through interaction. If you answer fan queries and engage with them, it will draw people to you. They will see you are in touch with treating fans how you would want to be treated by artists you like and this will paint you in a good light.

Establishing a connection with fans and showing an interest in them will grow your fan base and introduce more people to your music. It's not always about the music, some fans will want to know about you as a person too!

One of the best ways to get fans engaged is through competitions. Ask them to post parodies of your songs or design some kind of artwork for you that you will use in the future. Little things like this will generate a lot of interest in you especially if they get shared via other people's news feeds and thus to a broader audience. They can also spark useful ideas and potential material that you can use, along with making fans feel a part of something.

Key is always remembering to keep your posts interesting and engaging.

FACEBOOK ADVICE

One of the first steps in using Facebook is to make sure your bio, picture and information are as clear as possible. Also, make sure your profile picture on Facebook is the same or as near as it can be as the main picture used on your website and other social media to create a working synergy across all of your platforms. The same applies to colour themes and logos - you want to make sure that your style and imagery is demonstrated clearly to increase brand awareness. This all follows on to physical marketing and promotion.

Synchronise your social media
Use the same display pictures, backgrounds and names. Using the same imagery across all your social

media sites strengthens your brand as an artist. It looks more professional and official.

Using the same URL address name and sticking to it across all social media platforms increases your searchability as an artist, and makes it easier to find you on search engines such as Google. You'll need to customise your Facebook URL address as normally you will be allocated a series of random letters and numbers initially and this will not bring you up on search engines.

We live in an instant age and if you're difficult to find online people are easily distracted and move on, thus you could lose a fan who could have come to the next gig or shared your music to her friends.

Use similar URLs to increase searchability so they are easy to find. It may not always be possible to get all platforms the same but spending time to get this right from the start will be a huge benefit. Here's an example of the brand Open Mic UK's social media platform URLs:
Facebook: Facebook.com/openmicuk
Twitter: Twitter.com/openmicuk

On both platforms the main pictures are the same as are the backgrounds. It's a clear synergy leaving no room for confusion. It's important as an artist that you follow this formula.

It is sometimes impossible to have the same URL, for example if someone else takes it. If that is the case, try and keep it as similar as possible and the same across your social media platforms, for example openmicukmusic would be a good alternative.

FACEBOOK TOOLS

Using pictures, events and apps
Facebook is still one of the best marketing platforms for singers, musicians and songwriters to promote their music and events on. Facebook offers a very "real" audience and potential fan base for you and a network that allows you to share important information easily.

Facebook allows you to post information such as upcoming gigs, new music, videos, and so much more. Learning how to use Facebook to interact with fans and fellow musicians is very important. Despite the power of the Internet, using it effectively is not as straightforward as you'd like to think. It involves a lot of work but there are a lot of tools and tips that can help.

Post pictures
Post photos with your fans - gig pictures, meet and greets, anything showing you interacting with them! Ask fans to tag themselves, as this will promote your band to your fans' friends when the picture appears in their news feed.

Share pictures and videos! Fans are more likely to comment, like or share these updates as opposed to normal text posts. At the time of print videos posted directly on Facebook are receiving lots of encouragement as Facebook wants to take the market share of hosting video content away from rivals YouTube.

Create Facebook events for all your gigs

Create an event for anything you will be playing at or attending, so that could be anything from a gig to radio interview and/ or PR function. Even if the organisers have already made an event, make your own. Not all your fans will be fans of the organiser or venue in question.

Utilise Facebook apps

Utilise new apps! They are quick and simple and allow you to have elements such as music players, event listings and mailing list tabs on your Facebook page. The good news is that most of them are free! Some examples to check include Reverbnation and BandPage.

Keep your content engaging

Content is King so try to keep your posts engaging, interesting and/or funny and try not to do too many 'selly' posts whether it's the next gig or EP otherwise people will just switch off.

Always analyse your shares, comments and likes to see what's working best.

Network on Facebook

Networking with and reaching out to other acts is important when using Facebook as a singer. An unsigned act can acquire new fans by opening for another act on stage. The same goes for Facebook; ask another act that you get on well with to post your new music video/track/album art to their wall with a link back to your Facebook page, and remember to return the favour.

Another way you can really connect with your followers is to ask for input from fans. Ask yes-or-no questions (e.g. "What do you think of this picture for my album cover?") or pose multiple-choice queries ("Which song title is the most evocative?"). Gaining your fans' input makes them feel valued and part of your journey!

FACEBOOK CONTENT RULES

Post effective content
Getting your Facebook content right is important. Post too little and you are in danger of getting lost in people's news feeds and forgotten. Post too much and you will irritate your Facebook fans! Striking the right balance is essential in keeping your current fans engaged and growing your fan base.

Keep it to the point
Avoid the temptation to post overly long posts on Facebook; ideally keep statuses short and straight to the point. Of course you can be flexible with the amount of posts you do, for example if you have just released a record, are touring or are on the promotional trail then update your page more often, just so long as the content is of interest to your followers.

Use teasers to create excitement
If you've spent a long time and perhaps a lot of money making a new video, don't just put it up on

Facebook without ceremony. Try to create a 'teaser' campaign before you release the video. For example, posting behind-the-scenes photos the week before you release the video or short snippets of the video itself are good ideas for giving your fans exclusive content that will get them excited for the video. 'Coming soon' messages are a good way to increase suspense and pique interest. Similarly, if you have an album of loads of great photos from a gig, split them up into two or more albums and post them separately. Remember, photos are important; we have found that photos are consistently the most visited part of any act's Facebook page.

What are the best times to post updates?
The best time to update your page is when most of your fans will be on Facebook. A recent study shows that there are three times during the day when usage spikes: 11am, 3pm and 7pm. Updating on weekdays is far more effective than at the weekends when people are out of their regular routines. But of course as people realise this it can change the trend so watch what works for you, record how much activity you have and see if you can see patterns.

So a posting strategy of 11am on weekdays should get the best results. Take the stress out of it and schedule your updates with applications like HootSuite or Tweetdeck, which are tools that allow you to update a bunch of social networks in one go.

How not to use Facebook
Give self-promotion a break. Yes, the ultimate goal is to convert fans to support you financially through music, merchandise and ticket sales. However,

trying to push sales messages onto fans that already own your material or frequently attend gigs should be avoided.

A good ratio recommended by social media professional Steve Woessner is 6:1, that means six posts like 'this is what the act are up to' updates for every one selling something like 'and our new single is available from iTunes'.

Always interact

If someone has been compelled enough to make a post on you or your music, respond to comments and posts. Don't just push content onto fans and leave it at that; if they comment on your posts, reply to them. Facebook is a social network after all.

Always stay positive when responding to comments - avoid negativity and getting involved in arguments.

Good content takes time

Good content takes time to find, so perhaps ask friends for ideas. If you are struggling for ideas to post, try something different. It doesn't always have to be content directly related to your act. People may like your music but they will also be interested in your personality, style, opinions etc. Post videos, pictures and articles you find interesting. This will provide debate amongst your fans.

The reason some people have lots of followers is because they are funny and relevant so if you can, engage some measured wit and humour.

Reward your fans

People like free things, and if you give them free things, they will "like" you more. You shouldn't post your entire album free of charge and offer each fan free tickets for life, but throwing your social media followers something that they can't get anywhere else is a sure fire way to garner more fans (and keep the ones you have).

It's often forgotten but thanking people is actually quite a powerful way of reinforcing connections. When you're touring it's always good to post a thank you update after each gig. Even if just a small fraction of your total Facebook fans were at the concert in question, those fans will feel special for having attended and are likely to comment on your update, which will in turn publish to their own Facebook profiles.

Plan Facebook

So, to conclude, putting thought into how you are going to manage your Facebook page and being organised about what you want to say and when you say it will make your life easier and get the most out of your page.

As with all things it will need to represent your personality and it's going to take time but it's important to carve your identity. Perhaps in time a loyal friend, fan or family member could really help by assisting with running your Facebook page. Although it's a task that can be fruitful it can also be very time hungry to be done effectively.

TWITTER TIPS

Using Twitter to promote yourself

The rules on social media on the whole pretty much transcend across all platforms. So applying these rules discussed on Facebook to Twitter can be a big asset to you in building an effective fan base.

Have an objective

Always remember why you've got Twitter and how it can help you. Ideally as you are a musician you want to tweet about music but this isn't always possible. Keeping music as your focus will attract other like-minded Tweeters. The main key is to always make sure it is engaging and interesting.

Have a clear bio

It's probably going to be the thing that makes a follower decide to click on your account. Use fully that 160 character space to promote yourself and if applicable always have your website as your main link making it your hub of your social media strategy. Make sure your thumbnail picture is up to date, current and consistent with all your other social media and marketing i.e. all the same.

Interact with followers
Don't just talk about yourself; reply to messages or tweets, and make them personal! Everyone gets a little buzz out of being retweeted or replied to by someone on Twitter. People give up interacting with accounts that don't engage, so why not be the person that creates that buzz?

Use hash tags (#)
Hash tags are used to make the searching function easier, so using them in your tweets brings your account to more people's attention. So if you're going to see a band on their tour, why not tweet 'who else is seeing #ABand tonight?'

Don't post all the time
There is nothing more annoying than someone constantly spamming your feed with his or her incessant tweets. Don't post the same thing constantly; you'll end up losing followers.

Self-promotion is encouraged but not when it's the only thing you post. A good way of keeping interest in your account is to tweet regularly but mix it up. So post what you're doing today, something that made you laugh or just a picture you find amusing. Variety is the spice of life after all and monitor what sort of posts get more traffic.

Spread the word offline as well as online

You should remember that you would gain a bigger fan base by talking about what you do to people around you. Just because you're not logged in, doesn't mean you can't gain a few more followers. Put your username on your flyers, make sure people know you're on Twitter and they can find out more about you there.

As discussed before have consistency of the URL's with other social media platforms and the website is the hub of your social media brand.

USING YOUTUBE AND VIDEOS

Tips on how YouTube can help you

YouTube is the most popular video platform for singers as we go to print, although Facebook are keen to take a piece of this market, so uploading to both is a good idea as it stands.

Uploading videos of your performances makes sense as a singer; it's free, demonstrates visually what you can do, plus you can easily be found on the Internet if you title and describe your videos correctly.

Don't think your videos are going to be seen by millions, as it always takes a lot of time and hard work to build up views, so you have a little (well a lot of) work to do before that happens. However, start to get it right and your performance can be shared across a wide audience and in some cases artists have been signed on the back of publishing their videos.

Be creative

As always be different and don't sound like every other singer; you have to have something unique about your voice that makes people want to hear more. So if you're going to upload a cover, make sure you've made it your own. Try not to imitate other singers' voices; you have your own voice so make sure people know about it. As always make it engaging and interesting, something to stand out otherwise people will just move on.

Subscribe

Promoting your video is essential and as always building up a fan base is critical if you want to be scouted on YouTube. By building up your subscribers you'll have a basis of viewers as each video you upload will show up on their account.

Upload quality videos

Take time to get it right. It's great if you can invest in a camera with the ability to record a good quality video, but just getting the lighting, background and settings all spot on is far more important.

Don't upload anything unless you're 100% finished with it and you'd be happy for people to see that video in a few years time. Uploading unfinished videos is unprofessional and makes fans lose interest and you're not giving them everything you're capable of. People will judge your worst performances so it's best to always have quality in mind rather than quantity.

Tagging your video

One of the reasons some acts are discovered on YouTube is because they're tagging the words people are searching to their advantage. For example if you're uploading a cover, you're going to need to use a number of tags such as cover, music, artist's name and your name. The idea is to tag what people are going to have to search to find you. Making these terms as relevant as possible makes people finding you a lot easier.

Don't forget to complete the description on your video to include where people can find you so include your website and other social platforms.

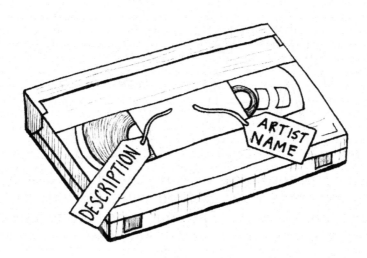

Seven

RECORDING

CHOOSING A RECORDING STUDIO AND PRODUCER

You've spent time and effort writing your own material, so when it comes to laying down your tracks, choosing a recording studio and producer that will share your musical vision is crucial! Here are our tips on finding the right recording studio and producer for you.

Listen to other singers' work and if you like it ask them who they have worked with. Get advice from fellow musicians to find out who produced their recordings and get a first-hand view on what the producer was like to work with.

Select a producer who has worked on similar music
Try and pick a producer with recording experience in your chosen genre or with similar music that you'd

like to produce in the studio. Where possible do the research - check out the music, the studio and what the producer has produced recently before booking studio time.

Be clear with your objectives

Before approaching them, make sure you are clear about what you want to achieve, and know what you want your sound to be. If struggling perhaps consider a mood board to take with you that includes genre/similar artists etc. to give the producer a firm idea of your vision.

Ask for samples of work

Ask the producer to send through samples of their work that is most relevant to your music.

Try and choose a producer within a reasonable location to save money, unless the producer has an impressive portfolio. It also makes editing the recording easier further down the line.

It is important you are confident with the producer. Ask yourself 'are they easy to deal with, and is their communication clear'?

RECORDING STUDIO PREPARATION

Preparing for the recording studio can save you valuable time and money. Making sure that you, and your material, are ready to record is vital for a focused recording session. Read on for our hot tips for preparing for the studio!

Have a clear idea of what you want the end product to sound like.

Song preparation

Decide, do you want the song to have backing vocals or any additional instruments? Making as many of these decisions as possible before you visit the studio is easier for the producer. Of course the plan can change but at least you have a plan and vision to start with.

If you want the song to be a commercial single try to keep the song length to no more than 3.5 minutes (the length of a standard pop song). Make sure in rehearsals you tighten the song to the length required for the recorded version.

In the song writing process make sure the song grabs you straight away with a catchy hook line (this can be an instrumental and/or vocal line). Most people will decide if they like a song or not within 30 seconds, so ask yourself questions like 'is the intro too long?' and 'does the song show off my sound and abilities best?'

Rehearse and practise

Make sure you have rehearsed your songs to perfection. The recording studio is not the place to rehearse, as you'll eat into valuable studio time!

Practise with a metronome

Practise your song with a metronome to avoid timing issues, especially if you are used to singing along live with instruments. It can really throw you if you come into the studio and realise you have got used to performing to your own timing, which is fine for live performances, but not when recording.

Rehearse your techniques! Vocalists should practise warm up and breathing techniques as studio microphones will pick up all nuances no matter how subtle. Guitarists should practise to avoid finger sliding squeak noises unless of course that's what you desire in the track and drummers should always bring spare sticks.

Prepare for the day
The night before recording, you need to make sure all of your equipment is set up properly and you have spares if you need them. Ahead of the day and on the day be prepared to tell the music studio exactly what you want from them; you're paying for their time so make sure you make the most of it. It's potentially going to be a long day, so make sure you're ready to work hard and focus on what you're doing.

WHAT TO EXPECT AT A MUSIC STUDIO

So you have finally chosen a studio! This is when the real hard work begins, so make sure that you show some recording studio etiquette.

Act professionally and listen to the producer. The quicker you respond and deliver what the producer needs, the more you will get from your session. If you are difficult to work with word could get around. If you impress and get on with the producer they are far more likely to be happy to pass your demo on to their own contacts in the industry.

As a singer it's important to make the most of any studio time. It's the place to finally record that well-rehearsed music you've perfected. Therefore taking control, communicating and preparing ahead of the day will give you the best chance of preparing yourself efficiently and will increase the chance of getting the recording you desire.

Communicate
Speak to the studio and establish whether your session comes with an engineer or not. Some larger studios will just rent out the studio and you will have to arrange an engineer in addition. In the main the producer will run the vast majority of studios, but it is worth double-checking.

Establish rates, times, availability and what equipment is supplied or not. If possible pop in for a quick visit and chat with the producer and ask for samples of their sound.

Have a plan
You must be organised and know what you want to achieve in your studio session and then translate that to the engineer, otherwise you will leave the producer guessing and the end product may not sound how you wanted it to.

Ask questions especially at the end of the session to make sure you understand the next steps and when you will get the finished product.

Listen to the engineer

Of course it's your recording session and it's your money that's being spent, so you want it to sound exactly like you imagined. However it's also wise to let the engineer direct the music too as they are likely to have ideas and experience that will help improve the songs. The engineer will be familiar with the sound from the speakers and the sound the studio creates and thus how the song will sound outside of the studio in general, so it's always important to consider their view.

Editing

Once you've got all of your music recorded, it then goes through editing. This can be a tedious process, and since you're probably paying by the hour it's best to make sure it's done quickly. Many people like to 'fix' parts of the music after it's been recorded; sometimes it's quicker just to sing it again, which will save you money.

Rehearsing and preparing as much as you can in the first place will help you save money because if you've perfected the song it reduces the need for lots of edits! Again there are never any short cuts.

Mixing

Mixing is when the song is tested through different outputs to see whether it has a good quality sound no matter what it's played through. It's sometimes wise to take the finished product home and see how you feel about it outside of the studio, then bring it back if there's anything you want changed with the arrangement or levels of each part of the track.

Mastering

Once your music has been edited and mixed, it then gets mastered. This is when audio levels, EQ and compression will be worked on.

If you are doing an album this is where the CD and its tracks come together; the order of the songs and the album sound are worked on as a whole.

Post studio

After any recording session, remember to back up all your work and test that you can recover it. There's nothing worse than having to go back to square one and having all that valuable studio time go to waste!

If you made it through all of our tips on preparing for the studio then you should be armed and ready for the recording studio.

Eight
PUBLIC RELATIONS

PUBLICITY

Why publicity is important
So you've got an EP or single recorded and/or you have important gigs approaching. Now you need to try and get word out there to the public so they are aware of this.

As with all things you'll probably be in the position to do it yourself to start with, but doing your own publicity will teach you and give you an understanding of the process thus giving you an appreciation of the effort that it can sometimes take.

Make sure it's newsworthy
Key to success is how newsworthy the news is, as this will make it a lot easier to sell. To start with approach local press - most cities and towns have at least one local paper, magazine and radio station.

In addition if you do the research there are likely to be lots more smaller media platforms too, like volunteer radio stations such as hospital and student radio. Even if audience numbers are small it is a great way of getting in some media training to obtain interviews with them. Often many of these radio stations will be involved with local events, so that's another good reason to be in contact and get involved as this may present an opportunity to perform.

The approach

Before you go gung-ho sending emails to all the local journalists and ringing them up every ten minutes, take the time to perfect your pitch about why you are contacting them.

'Hi, I'm a singer – can I go on your radio station please' is an example of how not to word an email or phone call. The journalist will have many approaches every day and most likely skim over it without giving it a second thought.

Your pitch needs an angle, or a story. Have you got a slot at a local festival, or an EP launch night? Use the best headline you can to try and grab the journalist's attention.

If you are applying for a radio interview, you may need recorded songs to be able to play to the listeners or they may want you to perform live.

PUTTING TOGETHER A PRESS RELEASE

You need something to back up your words explaining your story for your newspaper article. What you need is known as a 'press release'. This needs to be carefully thought out so it is written in a way to grab people's attention and make them take notice of you. Here's what the press release should consist of:

The first impression

Your first paragraph and title needs to catch the readers' attention. Get to the point and state your reason for getting in touch. The press will receive many more press releases like yours every day. Don't wait until the end to say 'Joe Bloggs is supporting Lady Gaga later in the year'. That needs to be at the top otherwise the reader may miss that point, as it's unlikely they will have time to read every line your press release contains.

Here's a way to perhaps NOT word that paragraph: 'Joe Bloggs has a new EP and will launch it at The Dog and Duck next week'. Try to grab the readers' imagination; perhaps a better way to word it would be: 'Norwich's hottest talent for years, being likened to the British Justin Timberlake, Joe Bloggs is gearing up for the launch of his new EP at what is set to be one of the events of the summer at The Duck and Dog next week!'

What a press release should include

If you have had a good selection of activity recently, include any details of it.

A brief bio, that is engaging and interesting, informative but perhaps including something throwaway that will tickle the reader like 'did you know Joe Bloggs can juggle 6 eggs in 1 hand?'

Throw in some quotes. If people have been saying you're a great singer, put it in there to back up your belief in yourself.

A recent photo you've had done, most ideally the same picture used on all your social media and advertising material.

Contact details: phone number, email address and social media web links. Make sure all contact details are on the last part of the press release and they are clearly labelled as such to the journalist. You don't want them to put all your contact details over the Internet by accident.

MAKING A PRESS RELEASE STAND OUT

Make your press release stand out from the crowd

A journalist will get loads of emails and calls each day all from people trying to give their story to them. They can't possibly report on all of them so your approach needs to stand out from the crowd to have a chance of gaining their interest. Here are a few ways to go about this:

Get a contact

Always make it personal; take the time to call up the publication and/or radio station to speak to the right person you need to be contacting. Get their name and check all details you have are correct. This simple phone call will allow you to introduce yourself and maybe leave an impression so they remember you when your email gets to them. Keep the conversation brief and to the point, as it's not uncommon that they will be working to a deadline.

After you send the press release, drop them a call to check they received it. Don't do this right away, but if you don't hear anything after a couple of days it may jog the journalist's memory to go back to it! Try and get a straight answer from them in regards to knowing if they will use your press release. Be careful to get the balance right between being keen and hassling them. They can be persuaded just like anyone, but equally they can also get easily irritated.

Always address the person you are contacting properly and professionally. Phrases such as 'Hey there mate' should be avoided. 'Hi there Paul' would be much better and more personal. This should keep them reading after they see their name.

Invite them to your gig
Making contacts and networking is vital in the music industry. Any people you send press releases to should be invited to attend your gigs or EP launches. This will help in future when sending press releases. They might even mention you to their contacts and spread the word.

Build a portfolio
Keep newspaper clippings and radio interview recordings, as they can be incorporated into future press releases and can certainly be used for your social media.

Make the most of the opportunity and post on your social media, before and after where applicable. Post links to any press you have done on your social networking sites. Ask your contacts to share it on Facebook or re-tweet it on Twitter.

Getting re-tweets or shares of links to your press articles will help get your name here, there and everywhere. This way the next time you gig, people in that area are more likely to have heard of you.

Follow up

Always send an email follow up thanking them for the article and/or radio interview; always include an invite to your next gig! You keep building and they will eventually come down to watch.

Of course once they have supported you once, nurture the relationship by keeping them up to date with your bigger events and outings. As long as you keep contact sparse and concise, there should be no reason for them to not keep reporting or interviewing you; as with everything just do it in the right manner.

RADIO INTERVIEW ADVICE

Smashing that radio interview

In a radio interview, you will undoubtedly be nervous the first few times if not every time. Nerves can make your voice appear tense or dull on air and the audience will pick up on this, so it's important to be aware and find ways to compensate.

The best advice would be to start gaining some experience by getting interviews with volunteer radio stations such as hospital and student radio, so you get a feel for the environment. Even if audience numbers are small it is a great way of getting in some media training. You can analyse after and look to improve and develop your presence on air.

Thereafter you should have the confidence and experience to expand; most local FM radio stations are always keen to support local singers and acts and some will even have unsigned shows; so get involved.

Preparation
Plan ahead if possible! Don't be afraid to ask for a glass of water beforehand. This will save your mouth drying out. Ask the presenter beforehand what kind of questions they will ask so you can prepare your answers accordingly.

Listen to the presenters' show ahead of the date so you are familiar with the show and the presenting style. Also listen to the presenter when at the radio station so you fully understand the questions Focus on the question in hand and not any future questions you will be asked.

How to talk
Be friendly and open. Use informal, everyday language. Talk as though you were talking to just one person and don't use any jargon. Keep to the point and avoid waffling. Emphasise important words, as this will make you sound more convincing.

Plan what message you want to get across and focus on it! If your new single is out next week, focus on that! If you have a show that week, make that your priority. Try not to over-sell the message; you don't want to be too one-dimensional or bore listeners.

If you're a group, make sure each member is on the same page. Try and get everyone involved at some point as opposed to having one member do all the speaking, or worse still you all answer questions at the same time, so plan an order of who is going to answer questions.

Stand out

Make yourself stand out! Grab the audience's attention. Maybe make a competition beforehand offering the winner a free copy of your EP or a pair of gig tickets.

Keep to sounding positive, fun and enthusiastic, avoiding sounding defensive. Simply stick to positive statements and never resort to negative attacks. Most importantly, relax and enjoy yourself. When you smile, your voice smiles and listeners will pick up on this.

Post interview

As with any media coverage always thank the presenter (or editor) and ask if you can come back in after a few months to give an update. After the interview, write a thank you email to the producer and the hosts. Tell them that whenever they'd like to have you back, you'd love to be a guest again.

Afterwards review the interview identifying where it went well and where it could be improved for next time. If possible ask for a copy and post on social media according to how it's come out.

PR COMPANIES

Things you need to know before considering hiring a PR company

It's best to hold on to doing your own publicity as long as you can but when the job is beyond you and there is a need for a wider coverage it may be time to consider a PR company (public relations). PR companies are there to help promote all manner of things but in the context of a singer it is most likely it will be for their single or album release. PR companies can gain wider promotion for news, releases and tour dates of an act to the media.

Choosing the right PR Company is essential. By following some of the advice below you could find a PR company hugely beneficial in getting your music career to the next level; however, get it wrong and you could just land yourself a large bill and nothing to show from it.

Research the PR Company
Before you consider hiring a PR company it's important to find out more about them as a company. Make sure you know what experience they have and what they can offer you as an act. If you can't find any information about them, it's not wise to hire them. Look for credentials and testimonials, reviews from past customers that have used them, so you can see who else they've worked with and if they're appropriate for you.

Don't pay too much up front
If a company is asking for a lot of money up front, before they've done anything for or with you, be careful. Be smart: try and get a trial run first so you don't pay over too much until they've completed at least some work that you're happy with.

In an ideal world, to start with you want to find a PR company that you pay as per results for each

125

successful piece of media coverage. Admittedly they are much harder to find, although I know a good one and I'd always recommend this.

Know what you want

You're considering hiring a PR company, so it's important you know what you want them to do for you. If you've already been doing your own publicity before this point it will become clearer. If you don't know what you want, then how are they going to be able to do that for you?

Be realistic

Have you built your act's presence enough to benefit from a PR company? There are hundreds of releases each week so you need to have built up your fan base beyond being just a local one to merit it, otherwise you will be just wasting your money.

Key is to be newsworthy; what's different?

Nothing is going to give you better knowledge than if you have tried to get PR yourself. You will then know what is possible and achievable. If you can't even get local press and media interested then how can you expect to get any publicity on a wider remit? As with all media coverage press will need to see it as newsworthy otherwise they won't publicise it.

Be available

Make sure you are easily available as your PR person could be setting up interviews for you and some opportunities may come up at very short notice. If you're unavailable or hard to contact it can be just a waste of everyone's time!

Nine
WHEN TO APPROACH STRANGERS

This title may sound flippant but giving your full consideration to this chapter could save you hours of time or even years; instead of wasting energy you could be on a path to a successful career in the music industry.

MANAGEMENT

What does a manager do?
All music mangers vary and can do an array of different jobs to help artists develop every aspect of their music careers. What a manager does for you depends also on what you want from them. So having a clear plan and good communication between yourself and your manager is key.

Always remember (and the clue is in the title) management are there to aid you, and it's certainly not the case that they are going to do everything for you. In fact it's more accurate to say that management are there to direct you on what to do, rather than do it for you.

Main jobs for managers
Every manager and agreement is bespoke but some of the main jobs for a manager relate to being the spokesperson for the artist. These can include management sending out demos to labels, radio stations, local print media, and online publications, book gigs and promoting the events to the public and

press. They can help organise studio time and practice sessions, the production of music videos and photo shoots. They can also network and talk to people about the artist and find as many opportunities for the artist as possible.

How to choose a manager

If you're quite early on in your music career you may not have the funds to afford a music manager, and management may not be interested in working with you at this stage until you have developed further into your career.

So some artists choose to bring a friend on board to help with managing their affairs. The good thing about using a friend is that they will (hopefully) have your best interests in mind and will have the same passion for getting your music heard as you do. However a friend may not have the music industry knowledge and contacts that you need to further your career and take you to the next level. Furthermore if things develop the pressure of them devoting their free time may come under strain, but on the flip side the possibility of having a hard working passionate person that you can trust on the team is always a welcome one.

Built on trust

The most important thing you need to consider when choosing a manager is your relationship with them. You need to be able to work with someone that you can talk to openly and honestly and have good communication with.

If the potential manager is a person you don't know then do some research, find out the kind of acts they have previously worked with and see where they are, what they are currently doing and what they have achieved. Don't just jump into something with the first manager you find; have a meeting and see how you feel you could work with them. Especially if it's your first taste of management ideally try and work with them for a month or two to see how the relationship develops; if you can't communicate effectively together to start with it's unlikely it will change down the line.

Give it a chance
If you are going to do a trial period with a manager, be loyal and don't court other interested parties. Be honest and try and build a relationship rather than wonder why a manager has lost interest; it's probably because they have worked out you're not committed or loyal to them. So you need to play your part in developing trust and a working relationship.

Do I need a contract with a manager?
YES! Even if you're with a personal friend and there is no money involved for now, you need to write up a formal agreement. It would be advisable to write a plan and an exit strategy should it not work out so that both parties know what's expected and what will happen if it doesn't really work out.

So jot down what is expected of both manager and act, what the percentage of income for the manager will be and what happens if you both decide to part ways. Many artists don't want to make their friends sign contracts, but when you're entering into a business relationship with a friend, a contract keeps the friendship safe.

DO ARTISTS NEED MANAGEMENT?

Certainly what I'd advise especially when starting out is just concentrate on your own affairs to begin with. Again you can't short cut doing the miles so learning or having some idea of what is in involved in most aspects of your career is vital knowledge.
Let management find you.

Don't waste time searching for management as the magic wand to sort out your career; concentrate on building your career to a level and management will find you! When you are a big enough deal you will find these opportunities will just open up easily.

In conjunction with the above point, once you have built up your career and are getting to the point where it's too much for you to handle all of the opportunities coming in, then it may be time to consider getting some assistance to guide you to the next level.

Reasons you may want management
Below are some reasons why you might want to have artist management. The most important thing when choosing to take a manager or not is that you get the right one, who understands you and is someone who you can have a good relationship with.

Managers can offer you the chance to focus on your music. They can take over any admin tasks you have which allows you to focus on making music and developing your career.

A good manager is one who has contacts and knowledge that can help you in your music career. The main reason for management to be a part of your career guidance is because they can probably see the 'bigger picture' that you may fail to notice and can help you achieve your goals with their industry know-how.

Some record labels don't give acts the time of day if they don't have management. Working with a reputable management company shows they believe in your act enough to support you and help you to progress in your career. The reason record labels don't like to work directly with the act is because they want to do business with someone who knows the music industry and won't have an emotional attachment.

WHEN DOES A SINGER NEED MANAGEMENT?

Some acts won't need management until a few years into their career. It's difficult to pinpoint the moment that you should start looking for management - if you're doing things right and you've built up your social media, gigs and fan base then management will find you.

Sometimes it's better to wait until you are at a stage in your career when you can't cope without help. All the time you don't have management you have the control, you book gigs, arrange tours, radio plays, sort out merchandise, you can do everything yourself. The only person that truly cares about your image and your music is you. As you become more successful it will just be too much for one person and will need a team at some point to support this workload.

Managers cost money. The vast majority of management deals are based on commission. That means that your manager takes a percentage cut of income you generate, so you need to make sure management is the right choice for you before you commit to giving away some of your income.

A guide to when is the right time for management

In short, management is a two way process: you may want to work with them but they might not necessarily want to work with you unless you are at the right stage of your music career. For management to want to work with you they are most likely going to need to see income streams already coming in or a strong indication that they are likely to. It's vital to have a strong, loyal fan base already built, otherwise management have to consider not only whether to take you on as an artist, but also the task of building a fan base from scratch, which in the vast majority of cases they won't be interested in.

You on the other hand need to see what doors and opportunities management can realistically get you. The timing is probably right when you need the following.

Career guidance

A time may come when management is needed to work with you to figure out what's next for you as an act and give a vision. The main reason for management to be a part of your career guidance is because they can probably see the 'bigger picture' that you may fail to notice.

Time management

Have you got to a stage where you're struggling to cope with all the work you've got to do? Are you putting your practice on the back burner to do other tasks that aren't as practical? This is the time to consider management, although depending on the tasks you could just employ someone rather than commit to management. However if you've got this much to do, at the expense of your act, then you need support and management may be the next step to take.

Making the right choice with management should allow these tasks to be done by them rather than you and allow you to focus on making music and developing your career.

You're looking to contact record labels

Many record labels will refuse to give an act the time of day if they don't have management. A reputable management company should already have a working relationship with record labels or they should know of each other. This of course should make it easier to get your music heard.

PUBLISHER

What are publishers?

Music publishers are also known as publishing companies. Essentially you only need a music publisher when you have written your own songs, so if you are still in the early stages in your music career a music publisher may not be necessary. Music publishers make sure artists and composers get paid royalties every time their song compositions are used commercially.

Publisher's contract

Through an agreement called a 'publishing contract', an artist/composer assigns the copyright of their recordings to the publisher for which they take a cut of what they collect. The company then licences compositions, monitoring when and where a composition is used, collecting any royalties and paying the artist. The publisher takes a percentage of the amount to cover its services.

Proactive publishers will promote commissions for the artists' compositions to be used by films, television, advertisements and other recording artists. They also seek out newer ventures to promote the music to, such as ringtones for phones.

They also take action on anyone using the music without the necessary licence.

The copyrights to compositions are one of the most important forms of intellectual property in the music business. The publisher's main role is to manage this asset on behalf of the artists.

How do royalties work?

After agreeing to a publishing contract, the music publishers will collect various kinds of royalties. They may pay the artist an advance up front if they can see there are royalties to collect and then take a percentage of the royalties, sometimes as much as up to 50%, but it's usually around 20%. There are a few kinds of royalties, which in the main fall into these categories:

Mechanical royalties

Mechanical royalties are from the sales of recorded music, such as CDs and digital downloads. This is what the record companies have to pay the music publishers.

Performance royalties

These royalties are collected by performance rights organisations such as BMI or Performing Rights Society (PRS), mostly from radio stations and live venues, who all have to pay to broadcast recorded music on their radio station or at their venue each time a song is played.

Synchronisation royalties

These are paid when a composition is played in a film or in a TV show.

Proactive publishers will also take songs by songwriters and give them to suitable recording artists to perform. They also try to get them included on film and TV soundtracks. They handle copyright registration and ownership issues for the artist.

FINDING A MUSIC PUBLISHER

Deciding who you want to publish your music can be an important factor for your future success in the music industry. Quite often if you are at the level of having management, they will usually advise and source a publisher for you.

Although a songwriter can certainly handle their own publishing, a good publishing company can be extremely helpful. However finding the right music publisher can be tricky, so below are some helpful tips on how to go about getting a publisher.

Create a demo
Creating a demo would be your first move. This simply means getting some of your material put into a hard copy that you can then distribute. It's essential that these demos are a high quality because the demo will act as the band's or singer's CV, so make sure it is well recorded and that it represents you well.

Sending your music direct to publishers
This is when the Internet is a useful tool; searching publishers may not be as easy as you would originally think. A wise thing to do is to search artists of the same or similar genre as you and find out who they're published by.

Once you've found some publishers you're interested in it's best to contact them to find out if they are happy to receive submissions and if so what format they want your demo to be in and who to direct it to etc.

Network

The best way to network is through contacts you have built in the industry, such as fellow musicians and singers at gigs and open mic nights. They may be able to give great first hand feedback of any experiences of whom they have used or currently use for publishing.

Go to music events and seminars where there could be publishers. So if you know someone important in the industry is going to be somewhere, make sure you're there too.

Like artist management, signing to a publisher is a two way process; you may want to work with them but they might not necessarily want to work with you. For a publisher to want to work with you they are most likely going to want to see income streams already coming in or a strong indication that they are likely to. So they may either want to see evidence of music sales so they can collect money straight away or see the potential in your music; without this they are unlikely to sign you.

WHEN DOES A SINGER NEED A PUBLISHER?

Essentially you only need a music publisher when you have written your own songs. If you are still in the early stages in your music career a music publisher may not be necessary.

The timing will vary; perhaps wait until you have a few songs, at least an EP's worth, or at such time as when you start to perform your songs at venues or have them played on radio as you may well be entitled to some potential royalties. Always keep a record of when, where and how long your song was played for as this may help in the collection of royalties.

Although a songwriter can certainly handle their own publishing, a good publishing company can help them take their career to the next level. The good thing is that publishers only get paid on what royalty money they collect.

The publisher signs the songs not the artist
Always remember that the publisher signs rights to the song to collect royalties, not you as an artist. In some cases the contract may allow the song to be offered to a different artist, so make sure you check what you are signing.

If another artist does have success with your song this can open doors for you, as an artist yourself and certainly as a songwriter. There are countless examples of artists becoming successful as a result of their songs being successful before them as an artist.

How does a publishing deal work? A proactive publisher
There can be two types of publisher. Some will just collect the royalty, and it is important to get someone who can do that effectively. But ideally you want a publisher who can do that and also can be proactive to help your songs get used commercially or help you get signed.

The best result is to get a good publisher that believes in your music so they are proactive with your music and well connected to get your music to the right people.

RECORD LABELS

Approaching a record label
First consider if this is actually the best move as on a number of levels it may not be and you can waste a lot of energy when perhaps it's not the right move for you at this stage of your career! So before you go gung-ho sending emails and making phone calls to record labels, there are few things to carefully consider.

Don't go too soon
Question to consider and ask yourself: is it too soon? How long have you been performing? You need to be sure you are ready and that you have a back catalogue of songs that are of high quality.

Make sure your live performance is up to scratch as generally if a record label executive is interested he or she may make a surprise trip to your gig. Are you at the stage of putting on a blistering live show or are you still developing and would they walk away thinking how you were rooted to the spot, singing out of key and generally looking lost?

Are you unique?
You need to be sure that the style you are going for is the direction you want to go. Are you unique - what do you offer to the music industry that's different?

When sending out your demo, is it of a high quality? Have you recorded it during a proper session at a studio? Is the song writing of a high standard or will the lyrics make no sense to whoever is listening?

If you think you meet the above criteria then you are maybe ready to begin contacting the record labels.

How will I know if I'm ready?
Very crudely: are you capable of making a sustainable living from music? Are you doing enough gigs, merchandise and selling music online to be a full time artist? A record label is unlikely to invest unless they see it working as a sustainable music business model that they can make money from or at least the potential, so it's essential you make this vision as close a reality as you can.

So if you are selling and getting booked enough that's a very good indicator that there is a demand for you and it might be time to consider selling your music to a broader audience.

Sending the demo
These days, record labels get inundated with demos. Let's not be under any illusions: this is a difficult route and you need to make sure you stand out so you don't end up getting skimmed over and discarded without a second glance.

You'd be best concentrating your efforts on one or two labels that you fit rather than bombarding all of them blindly...so do your research! Try and pick ones that have an affiliation to your style of music. If you a pop singer, sending a demo to a heavy metal label will clearly be a waste of time.

Always try and get a contact

Try and find out the name of the person you are contacting. It goes a long way to getting them to read the email you send. A simple 'hi there' will not draw their attention. They will assume you have just done a generic email sent to multiple people at once.

Include a brief bio that is engaging and interesting but perhaps add something a bit throwaway that will tickle the reader. Throw in some quotes. If people have been saying you're a great singer, put it in there to back up your belief in yourself.

Also include a photo of yourself, in line with your social media and branding. And of course contact details: phone number, email address and social media web links.

Be prepared that you may not hear back.

It's worth doing everything and sending off demos but in reality many may argue building up your own record sales, social media reach and higher profile gigs to network at will be more fruitful! Plus you'll hopefully be getting a return from the gigs and sales.

Is there a good time to send an email?

The timing of sending an email to a record label is very important! Some of this is fairly common sense but then common sense isn't very common.

Don't send it over a holiday or at the weekend. Monday morning will be when an email inbox is at its fullest, so chances are most emails will be skimmed over and discarded just to get through them. Wait until later in the week, maybe a Wednesday afternoon once things have calmed down.

Maybe try sending the email when you have good news to report. If you have an EP launch approaching or a slot supporting a well-known singer, it gives your email some clout and will make it of more interest to the recipient.

Keep all the plates spinning
Try sending a demo to coincide with you having some gigs lined up around the area where the record label is based and invite them to come down. This gives them a chance to check you out in the flesh as opposed to relying on your demo. Make sure the show is accessible so the record label has a genuine chance of seeing you.

This is no substitute for just networking which is far better than having to send blind emails. If you build up your fan base, music and all round buzz then labels will come to you. There is no substitute for doing the miles first and if you're good enough the opportunities will come.

HOW TO GET SIGNED TO A RECORD LABEL

Traditionally every unsigned artist is ultimately looking to be swept up by a record label and given the opportunity and backing to make it in the music industry. A record label can give you the investment in expertise and money to make you internationally renowned. However before they invest in the artist you have to show them why you are different and demonstrate enough potential that their investment is going to be a sound one (excuse the pun).

No rush
Before you approach a record label you need to make sure that you are completely happy with your music and the artist that you are. If you feel you need any further development, take your time and don't rush straight to a record label. If you go too early and not quite ready you may have lost your opportunity and when submitting material again you are likely to be dismissed as they will assume they have heard you before, making it hard to overcome that first impression, so hold back.

Don't dive into the deep end before you are ready.

How long should the demo be?

Demos should be kept short and sweet. Record labels get sent thousands of demos so they aren't going to listen to each demo for hours and hours. Pick your 3 best songs to showcase on your demo, making sure the first one is the best and is going to draw them in to listening further and then contacting you to hear even more of your music.

How to get scouted by a record label

Record label A&R scouts are always out and about at gigs and open mic nights searching for new talent to sign, so it is essential to get yourself out there performing live at as many gigs as you can as you never know who might be there watching you. Generally by learning and developing all the disciplines to a level as we have discussed is when it will start to come together and people will start talking about you. Start to make a buzz and many doors will open.

Presentation

Aside of what you do on stage it is also important you are presented in the best fashion so have a strong Internet presence. Many record label scouts will do their research online and so they are always searching the Internet for new talent. Make sure you have your best music up on SoundCloud and YouTube etc. Remember quality not quantity is key.

As detailed earlier in the book it is also essential that you have synchronisation in all of your social media platforms. So make sure your Facebook cover photo is the same as your Twitter header, and your SoundCloud display picture is the same as your website or YouTube display picture. Everything needs to be the same so you have a recognisable brand so that your fans and more importantly record labels can identify you
.

The same goes for your URLs, the more synchronised they are, the easier it is to find you.

What are labels looking for?

Record labels are businesses so they are after an artist that is going to make them money. Record labels have huge resources and are constantly trying to find the next big artist that is going to make it in the music market. So you need to make yourself unique to stand out from the crowd. In general the major record labels aren't looking for a copycat artist, as that is always going to be limiting on a number of levels, they want something different, so it's best to make yourself unique, which you are.

INDEPENDENT RECORD LABELS

An independent recording label is a label that is funded independently and isn't connected to one of the big major labels being Sony, Warner and Universal. Although an independent record label is a smaller company, they still have the ability to help musicians become big names in the industry. A smaller label can often mean more dedication to the artist, whereas with major labels you can get lost with the better more influential people at the label who will tend to work on the more established artists.

Often you'll find that an independent record label is a subsidiary of a major record label but independently run.

Be sure you are ready
Again to reiterate before you consider approaching an independent record label, you have to be realistic in whether or not you're ready. Remember that the music industry is a tough industry. You're not going to be considered by an independent record label if you haven't built up a big enough fan base, figured out your image or gained enough performing experience. You must remember the tortoise and the hare; don't rush and make sure you've done everything with consideration.

Most record labels are likely to want to see more than one song. Three potential hits songs is considered to be the back bone of an album; this gives the label more options which will improve your chances! So in most cases you are going to need a minimum of three potential hit singles you have written or collaborated on and a fan base.

Building a fan base as a singer
You will need a fan base: without them you'll struggle to go far and it will be very unlikely that any independent record label will consider signing you. The label will want to see a core audience demonstrated so they can see who would buy your products.

Approaching independent record labels

If you have the fan base, then make sure you have everything else lined up and sorted before you start approaching the record label. You wouldn't go to a job interview with half a CV so why approach an independent record label when you haven't got everything a label would expect you to provide.

Most labels will expect the basics demonstrated such as the following: a press pack, including the background to the act, music, social media platforms, website and any information to demonstrate an income stream. So make sure your CV demonstrates that you have the experience and all the tools to get the job.

Who to approach

Often independents can be quite niche so labels can be specific to certain genres, or work with certain acts, so do your research. This will help you to narrow down which independent record label you're most suited to and adapt your approach; in job interview terms let's call it adapting your CV to the job you're after.

Networking for a record label

Again perhaps work out when someone from the label will be somewhere, whether it's a seminar or gig, and try to talk to them at some point if you can; build up a contact. It will probably come across as refreshing to not give them a demo and instead say I'm preparing to give you a demo but only when it's ready.

Adele is a brilliant example of this, as she signed with XL Recordings in 2006 and is now one of the biggest selling artists.

Remember that being signed to an independent record label may not be the quick path to fame, but it's a great step in the right direction and could end up being the best career decision you make.

WHEN TO APPROACH A SOLICITOR

Stages when musicians need legal help

As you as a musician become more successful you may find yourself thinking 'when do I need a solicitor?' There are many times during your career when you may need a solicitor to help you with your music career.

In essence and the rule of thumb is if an agreement is offered to you then get it checked out before signing; however be aware agreements can be made verbally and via email so be conscious if things start to get a little formal and don't be frightened to ask questions.

Below are some stages when you'll need to seek legal advice! Make sure the solicitor is a music industry specialist and ideally comes recommended.

A solicitor works for you

A solicitor will always be arguing your corner and for your best interests for the deal, which can often mean they are to the point and a little aggressive at times. This can lead to a misinterpretation of the relationship and misjudgement of the nature of the intended agreement. So be mindful that it can cause potential irritation or even worse conflict and the solicitor should be working for you and not against what you want.

On the flipside it's important you don't take correspondence from the other party's solicitor too personally as he or she will be doing the same for their client. Make sure you keep communicating with the party you are dealing with as it can be difficult for the other party to interpret communication as coming from you via the solicitor. So be sure to be in control or risk alienating the party you actually want to sign with and potentially losing the deal.

Before signing your agreement

Firstly if you've started writing songs in collaboration with other writers this is when you may need a solicitor. Depending on what level you are at just a simple agreement between the writers as to how to share royalties is a good and sensible idea. You both sign it and you know in principle what is agreed on paper rather than what you both think, which later down the line potentially could cause issues.

Splitting song rights

If you can't decide, a solicitor will be able to help you decide who owns the copyright, who gets what percentage of royalties and who owns the stage name. Having said that song-writing organisations such as PRS and MCPS give guidelines based around splitting song ownership this may crudely cut as 50% melody and 50% written lyrics. If of course one or more people have written and contributed to the melody and lyrics you will have to pro rata the percentages.

As said it would perhaps be a lot cheaper to agree these guidelines and percentages without the need for a solicitor, as it will save money and really it only needs to be formalised if the music you have written is going to be used commercially.

Where agreement cannot be made the solicitor is potentially someone who will be able to advise and draft agreements. Just be aware technically you will need a different solicitor for each party i.e. everyone who contributed to the song, otherwise this could be a conflict of interests and of course this potentially can mean an increase in what you have to pay in solicitor fees, although many larger firms may be happy to draft in a colleague to assist.

Before signing to a publisher

You've started writing songs and have been presented with a publishing agreement. This is the time to contact a solicitor. You'll be looking for a publisher to help you find the best deal for your songs. A solicitor will help sift through the deal seeing whether it's appropriate to the songs you are writing and the terms are in your best interest.

Before signing to a manager

You won't need a manager until you've established yourself well in the music industry, but when that happens it's likely a few management companies will start to approach you. As discussed earlier don't rush into it and just get to know the management company first and who at the company you will be dealing with on a day-to-day basis.

Be cautious and don't rush into things just because you're excited about the opportunity. Explain to the company you want to make sure it's the right decision so you want to take your time.

However as soon as you are comfortable and you receive an offer, get a solicitor involved. There have been times when not having a solicitor read over the contract has left an act paying out to management even after they've left the manager.

Before signing to a record deal

A record label has approached you, the label wants you to sign a deal and has offered you a solicitor to work on the deal. Don't agree to this, get your own solicitor.

The chances are that solicitor wants what's best for them rather than what's best for you. You need to have an independent solicitor and one that will have your best interest in mind. In many cases the label will offer to cover both parties' solicitors' costs but of course every deal is different.

Ten

PERFORMING TO THE OUTSIDE WORLD

Singers need performances as a way of gaining more experience and performing on stage. Without any experience it's difficult for a singer to gauge which songs work well for an audience and which don't. Performance experience is an invaluable skill to have as a singer as it can often be a way of getting recognised by a wider audience. Most importantly performance develops your stage craft.

THE IMPORTANCE OF GETTING MUSIC GIGS

How playing at music gigs can benefit a singer
Playing gigs as with any performance is one of the most effective ways of getting recognised in the music industry, getting your music heard and building your fan base. As so many people attend music events, there is potential to play for a lot of people, providing you with great exposure if you impress.

However, ensure you are ready to play at a recognised music venue first; it may pay to do quite a few local open mic nights to learn stage craft and build the confidence before going in at the deep end.

Perform as much as you can
Gigging is one of the best things to have on your CV as a singer, as it shows you're willing to make an

effort. Also if you impress at a gig it's most likely to lead to more opportunities such as getting asked to play at other gigs. Many people in the music industry will look at your website and social media to see where you're performing next and of course the people you've impressed previously. It can only look impressive if you have list full of gigs and events coming up.

Always ensure you have leaflets and/or CDs so people can take your details or listen to you on the drive home and it's also essential that you are searchable on the Internet.

Word of mouth
Word of mouth is a powerful thing for an artist. All it takes is a few people to be impressed by your performance and to tell their friends about you and that gets the ball rolling of expanding your fan base. The more often you play, the more often you increase your chances of this happening, providing you are impressing with your music and performance.

Collaboration opportunities
The more often you gig, the more you will perform with other acts. One of the best ways to get noticed in the industry is to collaborate with other artists. So use gigging as an opportunity to make friends with other acts who would be willing to work on music and other gigs together.

Allows you to network
You never know who will end up coming to watch you play a gig, so it's smart to go and network after your

set is finished. Talking to everyone will give you a good reputation as well as giving you the opportunity to talk to someone who might have contacts that could be beneficial to you.

Selling merchandise

Getting regular gigs also allows you to sell your merchandise to existing and possibly new fans. All it takes is someone to buy your EP and share it with his or her friends to widen your fan base.

Selling merchandise is also another way of getting an income stream. This doesn't have to be limited to your music; clothing such as T-shirts, works of art, badges, basically anything you think will be of value to someone.

Create a mailing list

To do this you will need to design a leaflet to take details of people's names, emails or mobiles to add to a mailing list. You should do this every time you gig. If you gig enough, you'll soon have a good amount of fan information that you can use to advertise your new songs, gigs or news updates quickly and cheaply to a large number of people in one go.

OPEN MIC NIGHTS FOR SINGERS

How to utilise open mic nights as a singer

They may not be quite on a par with an actual gig, but playing at an open mic night will have its benefits for you. Your best bet would be to scout out which venues in your local area host the events, then try and attend maybe one or two every week. It may come at a small cost, for example petrol expenses, but if you are serious about a career in the music industry then it is something that must be done.

All open mic nights are run slightly differently; some may want you to pre-confirm a time, others will have a board to put your name up, some will have musicians as backing and others will be one song per act at a time and anything up to 30 minutes each act. So keep an open mind and go with the flow.

You don't get paid
You don't get paid – this is true; however, to actually start making money from playing shows you need to develop your stage craft and build a solid fan base. This doesn't happen overnight and local open mic nights are the first place you should be hitting to build up your presence in the local area.

There potentially won't be many people there, but you can use this to your advantage. It gives you more opportunity to interact with the people there and get used to being watched by a crowd if you haven't done any proper gigs yet. It's all practice as you develop your ability to perform your songs live without the opportunity to stop and start like in a rehearsal.

Open to all styles
People at open mic nights don't tend to be avid fans of any particular style. So don't worry about people not liking your style of music. Quite often there will be a variety of musical styles on show.

Quite often your audience will be made up of fellow musicians. This is a double-edged sword. Sometimes, supporting each other with compliments can lead to building a rapport and potential gig partners in the future. On the other hand, musicians can be the hardest people to please at times. Hopefully this happens rarely, but some people will spout negativity to make themselves look better if they see someone as a threat. If you come across people like this, just ignore any negativity and avoid giving any stick back. Show yourself to be the bigger person.

Showcase new material
You have the opportunity to showcase new material and see how it is received. After your performance you could ask for any feedback for consideration and make any additional changes to the song to give it more appeal if you agree. You could use the opportunity as a chance to write a proper set list, so you keep the best received songs in and remove any that didn't get much of a reaction.

Develop your stage craft
Use this not only for your music, but also for your performance skills. Interact with the crowd between songs to avoid any silent patches. This doesn't mean jump around like a loony running amongst the crowd, just the simple things. For example, not putting your hands in your pockets during vocal breaks.

Practise being confident and combating any nerves. Avoid having any kind of arrogance, as you don't want to potentially annoy fellow musicians who could end up being good contacts on the gig circuit.

Network

Use the events to network. Try different open mic nights all over your area; don't just stick to the same ones. Speaking to other singers and acts will hopefully open up more performance opportunities, shared gigs, promoter details and other gig opportunities.

If you need to find a musician to accompany you or to assist in song writing again open mic nights can be a good place to find talented musicians.

At the end of the day all practice is one step to being tighter when performing live.

SINGING COMPETITIONS

Ways in which talent shows can be used to help a singer's development

Many singers choose to enter talent shows as a way of getting noticed in the industry or for exposure to a wider audience. They can be a strong way to develop as a singer; here are some benefits of entering a talent show or competition.

Receive constructive feedback

Acts are generally given feedback on how the performance went or you can certainly ask. This is one of the strongest ways to develop as a singer: to know which parts of the performance are strongest and which bits need a little work. This is where competitions and talent shows can be really useful.

Receiving feedback from music experts who have a wealth of knowledge regarding the singing industry is a vital tool for self-development as a singer. Singers can use this feedback to work on. It's wise to take this feedback on board, as the judges will have experience and knowledge in the industry.

Building your fan base
Performing well and impressing on stage will help build your fan base. Audience members will take note of your details and find you on the Internet; so make sure you are easy to find on the Internet.

Getting exposure
A singing competition is often a chance for industry professionals to see you performing. With many competitions inviting A&Rs from record labels, management and people that work in the industry in general, there is a chance that the young singers are given further opportunities as a result of the attendance of these professionals.

It may only take an A&R from a record label to see a singer perform to want to learn more about them. Sometimes all it takes is the right person to attend a singing competition and give you the exposure you need to become a success in the music industry.

Builds confidence

Entering a singing competition can be a good way to help build confidence. Naturally there'll be nerves, but we all thrive when we're doing something we enjoy, and if you're a singer then performing on stage to a live audience is a feeling like no other.

Everyone gets stage fright, but the more stage experience a performer gets, the better they learn to handle those nerves. A singing competition is a good platform to gain stage experience in a safe professional environment. You will be surrounded by others in the exact same position so there is a great support network for them too and by the nature of the competition everyone will want you to do well.

Opportunities

When acts get to the level that they really impress they will then start to get opportunities like being asked to perform at other gigs and events, which are great opportunities for further exposure and/or management and record companies.

Singing competitions for children

Many children have dreams of being on stage and becoming a singer, but the music industry is a difficult place to break into, especially without performance experience. Places for children to sing and perform are limited but singing competitions give children that chance to gain experience performing in front of an audience and on stage.

Performing in front of an audience is vital experience for any aspiring professional singer, so many industry professionals will expect nothing less when looking to sign new talent.

Overall there are so many massive names that have made it in the music industry that have used competitions to develop and springboard their careers. So competitions can be a great resource to improve to the level to be successful.

MUSIC GIGS - HOW TO SECURE GIGS

Learning how to get music gigs is one of the most important things to master if you want to succeed in the music business. Live music gigs are integral for getting your music heard by the right people, giving them something they can't get from a studio recording – your raw talent and energy! Gigs are also instrumental in building up a fan base.

Compile a venue list
Compile a list of all venues in your area. Don't just stick to the venues most played at. Smaller venues such as pubs, bars etc. are maybe more likely to book an unestablished act, which gives you the opportunity to build your fan base and get your music heard. This will increase the likelihood of getting booked to play larger venues.

Be organised and include as many contact details of the people taking bookings as possible in a database. Name, address, phone number(s), email addresses! This reduces work time in the future and gives you a point of reference for the future.

Approaching venues

Now you've got your comprehensive list of venues and contacts, the next step is to start sending your press kit and demo to as many gig venues as you can.

Phone each venue and ask to speak to the manager or booking manager. This way you can ask who is best to send your email or press kit to.

Forward your press kit. At its simplest, this should contain: your contact information, links to all social media pages, a brief biography, the music you play and your experience. This will aid the venue to see what music you play and see where you have played before. It's best to include a photo and demo wherever possible. Remember to keep it simple and engaging and preferably concisely on one page.

When emailing, keep it short but factual (two short paragraphs)! No time for waffling as you will lose the venue's interest.

Foremost the venue want to support local musicians but their main priority is also to keep the business going so they are going to be attracted to booking acts that will bring energy and more importantly people into the venue.

Networking for music gigs

Not all venues you contact will lead to anything! In fact the vast majority won't, so don't get disheartened. Even if only a few get back to you, it's time well spent and at least you've got your name out there.

Getting those first few shows is most important. You can quote playing these venues when applying for future gigs! As you improve, most gigs will present themselves with more opportunities. Getting regular gigs to start with is the hardest part.

In the meantime, it's time to get networking

Attend as many gigs and live music nights as you can. Try and perform at open mic nights. This will give you experience playing to a crowd and you will meet like-minded people. Befriend other musicians, especially local ones. They can suggest venues, introduce you to their contacts and maybe even offer you to play with them.

Ask more established artists if you can open their show for them! This will get your music to a larger audience. Of course, you may have to repay the favour.

Social media

Use social media as a tool to make first approaches to other artists, promoters and venues. Thereafter try and meet up with them at their next event or gig.

There are also websites that can help you connect with other artists and at the time of print one such website, BandWagon, offers a service as the middleman between promoters and bands. Promoters list any gigs they are putting on that require extra acts, and members of BandWagon can apply for them.

GETTING SUPPORT GIGS

Targeting headlining performers for support slots

Supporting a bigger performer than yourself is a great way to get your music heard by a much larger audience and to expand your fan base. Obviously this doesn't mean go emailing Lady Gaga and Beyoncé trying to get on their tours as it very likely to be a waste of time.

Firstly start with singers/bands with a good local following who are of a similar style to your music.

Finding the gig

This is where the networking and having the ear to the ground is very handy. Check for upcoming shows in your local area. Figure out which shows you can make and find out if they have already announced their support acts. If not, get in touch and offer your services.

Going to their gigs, local events and open mic nights can be one way to network for contacts and other acts.

Who to approach

For smaller, more local shows it is often the promoter who puts acts forward for support slots. Having a good reputation, both in terms of fan base and performance level, will help you here.

Usually the good promoters who put on bigger shows in your area are the ones who deal with bigger acts, so try and get on the bill of some of their smaller shows and get known by them.

If you haven't had any shows with the promoters, get in touch for them and give them your details. Always be prepared for an act to drop out at the last minute so you get the call to step in. It could be the show that moves you up the ladder.

Another avenue is to try to find an act's booking agents and/or management contact email. Contacting them directly, without getting pushy or forceful, can help build up a rapport on a personal level.

Why should they pick you for a support slot?
An artist in the position to pick their support acts probably gets a fair few requests. You need to make yourself stand out. Ideally you do that by word of mouth and a reputation that you are not only good but also have a fan base. Either way you may need to make them check you out rather than press delete without giving you so much as a glance.

The key to getting the gig is that they will want an act that can boost ticket sales and warm the crowd up for them. You need to prove that you have the fan base and stage performance that can do this.

Making the most of your support slot
Now you have your slot on the bill, you have to put on the best show you can to win over new fans and leave a good impression on the headliners.

Fulfil any promotional commitments you make. Plug the show to your existing fan base and in the local area to generate interest and look to boost sales. This will leave a good impression on the headliner and the promoter if you are actively driving ticket sales.

Use the opportunity to write a press release and get more exposure for the event and yourself.

Sort out technical aspects of the gig in advance. Inform the venue of your set up and what you intend to bring. Make sure you know what time you are in for load-in and sound check. If you work full-time make sure you make appropriate arrangements well in advance if you need to take an afternoon off. Always get there early! Being fashionably late will do you no favours. If appropriate for your act, always ensure you have spares, such as batteries or guitar strings.

Find out if you can sell some of your own merchandise. It's better to ask than just assume you can! But always best to have it in the boot anyway so it's to hand.

Always be respectful to the sound engineer; they after all are the one responsible for your sound so always stay polite! Inform them of any visuals or unusual technical requirements you have.

Write a tech spec
Writing a small tech spec to hand to the engineer on arrival is always a good idea; make it clear and

concise, even if short to start with. Hopefully this will evolve to be adapted to any setting.

Always thank the promoter and sound engineer after the gig; you never know when you may need to call upon them again.

HOW TO GET FESTIVAL SLOTS

Tips on how to make festival organisers book you

As you become a more established act, naturally you'll want to start playing to bigger crowds. That's where sometimes festivals can come in, although they come in a variety of sizes, from basically glorified village fetes to ones the size of cities like Glastonbury.

Research

Before you start sending emails to everyone you've ever heard of in the music festival industry, do your research! Don't waste your time trying to contact people who may actually have no relevance to what you want. For example don't approach a festival for heavy metal or folk music if that isn't your music.
Instead, take your time to compile a list of useful contacts that could help you get your foot in the door. Find out when to apply, as for a seasonal event festival organisers often start booking months and months before.

Start locally

It's unlikely that any of the well-known festivals are going to book you if you have little or no experience playing at other festivals. The most realistic move for you is to look at local festivals. They'll be more likely to book local talent as it brings in local people and buzz, so you're in a better position.

Most local festivals have an application form on their website, where you can apply; these are only open for a short period of time, so it's wise to check them on a regular basis. As we said before, use networking and media contacts like local radio stations, for possible opportunities to getting that festival slot.

Keep it personal
Remember that festival organisers receive hundreds of emails asking for slots at their festival, so make sure you've looked into the festival you're applying for. Do research into each stage and find which one suits you best. That way they'll be aware you've done your research and they're likely to give your music a listen.

As always keep the email concise and to the point - two short paragraphs should ensure that it's not quickly looked over; you don't want to be one that a busy promoter thinks he or she will look at that later but never does. Also don't send attachments especially ones that are big files as you could potentially aggravate the festival promoter before they've even listened or looked; a simple hyperlink to a YouTube video can do the job just as effectively.

Send live examples

You're applying to play live at their festival, so send them your live videos. Show them exactly what they can expect if they decide to book you for their festival. Again keep the email approach easy on the receiver's eye; hyper-linking the sentence with your video link helps to keep it tidy.

As a suggestion if you haven't got any live stuff recorded, maybe approach local universities or colleges and ask for their media students to record you at a gig, or post a listing on local websites such as Gumtree. There'll always be someone keen to update their portfolio and record you.

Eleven
MAKE IT ON YOUR OWN

THE INGREDIENTS TO MAKE IT

There is no definite way to make it in the music industry, but there are a few ways to increase your chances of making it happen. Following some of the tips below may help you get a few steps closer to making it in the music industry.

Having talent
Yes it's obvious that you need to have talent to do well in the music industry, but being talented may not be enough. Being able to sing and perform is of course is the main part of making it as a singer in the industry, but there is always room for development and improvement.

Singing lessons
Many singers make the mistake of thinking they don't need singing lessons because they can sing. Singing lessons can help a singer to develop their voice and teach them tricks on how to use it effectively. Even established singers will continue to

have lessons to maintain their vocals and ensure bad techniques don't creep in.

Motivation and ambition
You aren't going to get very far in the music industry if you don't have any motivation or ambition. Assuming you're going to make it isn't going to be enough to be successful in the music industry. It'd be foolish to believe everyone is going to want to sign you, but for everyone that rejects you, there are others who might want to give you opportunities; but only if you have the motivation to put yourself in the right situation.

Act image and synchronisation
As an act you have to have the whole package: right down to your style choices and social media artwork, it needs to be uniform and consistent. Your image and music is core to you being successful as an act and they must therefore reflect your personality. Your image should complement your music and hopefully make you stand out too.

Marketing knowledge
Understanding how to market yourself as an act is one of the most important aspects of making it in the industry. You want people to know who you are, and marketing is the best way of achieving this. A common mistake made by singers is that they rely on social media as the basis for all of their marketing. This isn't enough. You need more than social media as not everyone is going to connect to you on there, so get out and spread the word yourself. Perform live as much as you can, sell merchandise, get on the radio etc.

Get lucky

This isn't really a tip but it's one way of making it. Being in the right place at the right time has worked for some singers. Putting yourself out there more will increase your chances of getting lucky in the industry. One thing is for sure though, the harder you work the luckier you will become, but of course work hard but work smart!

HOW TO HAVE A SUCCESSFUL MUSIC CAREER

Having a successful music career is not an easy thing to achieve; there can be many obstacles that stand in your way. The most essential things to any successful career is having good material, the personality to engage on stage, a fan base and a shed load of energy to create opportunities. So with that in mind the following will assist you on your journey to success.

Upload your material on social media

Starting with the basics, you're going to need a platform for fans to be able to find you on. So make sure you've uploaded your material on the likes of YouTube, SoundCloud, Facebook, etc.

These are the places fans will come to find you

Of course ensure the material is the best it can be and is professionally recorded. You need to have your own website and have all your social media pages directing to your website, which is one main platform for fans to find all the information they need about you.

Appreciate your fans

Make sure your fans know you appreciate them! After all, they are a large part of your success in the music industry. You can do this simply by responding back positively to comments on your social media sites, accepting friend requests on Facebook or following them back on Twitter. At events spend time talking and engaging with them, after all they have just spent time watching and listening to you.

Learn to perform

It's vital that you can sing well, but it won't be enough by itself. You need to be able to perform. Being able to perform will be one of the main factors that takes you from an unsigned artist to a recording artist. Most important is conveying personality and emotion in your performance. Many established acts will be the first to admit that they aren't the best singers, but what they lack in the strength of vocals, they more than make up for in personality and charisma on and off stage.

The key aspect to performing effectively is putting emotion into your performance.

Accept rejection and move on
You're not always going to have an easy job becoming successful; you're likely to face rejection on a number of occasions. It's in these moments that you'll have to accept you're not for them and move on. Don't ever give up, and keep going.

Remember, the Beatles were turned down plenty of times before someone gave them a break.

A good tip for acts is to ask for feedback and evaluate what feedback you get; take it on board if you agree with it.

Network
Develop your ability to network and build contacts. Networking is an important aspect for singers to work on, as it can be invaluable. With events being held specifically for networking, the concept has never been so important.

BE PROFESSIONAL

Tips on how to act as a professional in the music industry

Manners matter in the music industry just as much as they do in everyday life and knowing how to become a professional singer can set you apart from other acts at performances. It can leave a standing impression and make people feel more compelled to help you out.

Be on time, every time

Rule number one in how to become professional is to be on time – or even better, be early - for any event. There can be a lot of potential obstacles on the way to a performance including traffic, parking, getting lost and delays to public transport, to name a few.

You can always grab a drink and chill if early, so get in good habits and allow extra time when setting off. Music performances often run on a time schedule, so if you're late it can be difficult for them to cater for your tardiness. Being late is something that people remember and isn't going to help you.

Be respectful

Everyone is in the same boat when it comes to performing so be respectful to each act, regardless of his or her attitude. During sound check, applaud them when they leave the stage and when they are performing live. Stay quiet backstage during the performance and be friendly before and after their songs. Treat other people as you'd like to be treated. It can be a source of calming the nerves and even a confidence booster to be around friendly musicians.

Make people aware

A wise thing to do is to make the venue and organisation staff aware of anything out of the ordinary. This could be any guests attending who need special seating, or any unusual instrumentation you want to carry on stage before you play.

Organisation is so important before, during and after a performance. This also means that if you are unhappy with your sound check, let the engineer know and you can tweak your sound before the real thing.

Stay professional

Professionalism is something that sets apart acts during performances. If you are waiting backstage, try and refrain from cursing or entertaining other bad habits and stay where you are asked. Let your attitude show on stage, not elsewhere.

Please and thank you

It should go without saying that general manners such as saying please and thank you are very well regarded. Venue and organisational staff are working and taking time out of their day to help put on this performance so shake hands at the end of the day. It is possible to form working relationships with industry contacts this way and they will remember you for your manners next time around.

CORE BASICS FOR UNSIGNED SINGERS

It's important to remember all artists were unsigned at one point, so don't give up: keep working hard!

The key is to work hard, then work even harder! The harder you work the more opportunities you will create as long as you work smart. So once your talent has developed to a level remember to focus on the basics.

Be yourself

As singers of course you have influences and other artists who inspire you to carry on and pursue a career in music, but don't copy them. The idea of record labels is to find the new best thing, not a new copy of someone people already know.

Stand out

Being different will help you stand out, make people take notice before you even start to sing and perform; make them want to be interested.

Create a fan base

Fans are going to be the people that help you get success, so make sure you have a lot of them. Without fans there's no one to create a buzz about you as an artist! The best way for you to build up a fan base is to make sure you engage with them, respond to their comments, say thank you for their positive comments and post regularly.

Of course being really good on stage wins new fans and builds the buzz around you. Gigs and social media are your tools to build your fan base.

Love social media

It's one of the only tools that will help you stay relevant, so learn to love it. It's an easy way of getting the word out, along with compiling a list of people to email. Social media is a great way to show off your new video to all of your subscribers with a couple of clicks of a button.

With the likes of Facebook, Twitter and YouTube becoming increasingly important to the music industry, as an artist you'd be foolish not to use them

179

to your advantage. It's important that you keep a synergy between your image on stage and across your social media so your brand is consistent and professional.

Gig regularly

Make sure you're a known name at your local venues; you never know who's going to turn up to one of those open mic nights. Gigging regularly also gives you a sense of who you're trying to target your music at and which songs work with the audience. Again, work hard to promote any gig that you organise or a promoter gives you. Promote before, during and after. Be creative with the promoting and make each gig unique.

Take merchandise everywhere

Make sure you have merchandise and promotional material with you everywhere you play. It's an idea to give out your demo CD for free. Everyone loves a freebie and you never know: the guy who got dragged along to see you play might end up listening to it on repeat. At the very least have leaflets to hand out.

NETWORKING

Making contacts in the music industry

Networking is an opportunity to speak and connect with people who you may have never had the chance to before. For musicians it's an important skill to have as there are many useful people in the music industry with vast experience that can help you get to where you want to go.

Know your purpose

Remember why you're there and why you want to speak to people. At gigs or events try and target the people who are in the industry or have contacts that are. It's best to know exactly what you want these people to know.

Ask questions

When speaking or emailing contacts it's best to ask questions as it keeps the conversation flowing and also allows you to learn more about the contacts. The more you understand about the person the better the relationship you build.

Think outside the box

When you're trying to maintain contacts don't just keep and contact those people in your industry. Remember there are people and businesses as a musician you'll forever need. For example, you're going to need artwork and things like leaflets and business cards.

Follow up contacts

When you've made new contacts from gigs, now is the time to make sure they remember you. Don't waste the time you spent talking to them by not contacting them afterwards, even if it's a simple email expressing how nice it was to meet them.

The best way to ensure their response is to do it soon after they give you their contact details and to ensure your grammar and spelling are correct.

GETTING NOTICED IN THE MUSIC INDUSTRY

Ways to break into the music industry as a singer

It isn't the easiest thing to get noticed in the music industry, but there are simple tricks to making it a little easier.

Play anywhere

Firstly, you can't be too picky about where you want to play your music; if someone is willing to give you time to perform, take it. Any experience is good experience, so try to get regular spots at venues, as it will help increase your visibility locally. Playing at a variety of different places also helps you to realise what type of crowd you attract to a venue and can help you alter your performance accordingly.

Get a marketing team

Once you've got to a level try to start to build up a team of people who are willing to help you. Like a marketing team, this group can help you use social media effectively as an act and encourage the right kind of visibility. Another thing to focus on is a promotion strategy; there are clever ways to market yourself to your fans and potential fans and developing a strategy will help focus your efforts.

Create a press pack

Of course you want to be successful and have record labels sign you, but like a person applying for a job, you need to have a CV. As an act your press pack can act as your CV. This is the portfolio that contains everything about you as an act.

A press pack will include things such as your demo CD, a background to the act, styles and influences, a typical set list and a high quality photo.

Learn to self-promote

With the Internet being so important, you'd be silly not to use it to promote yourself as an act. Therefore learn how to use each social media platform, and interact and chat with your fans. These are the people that will help you to become successful after all. Make sure you have artwork that can be used to help increase your visibility too.

Synchronise your social media

Use the same display pictures, backgrounds and names. Using the same imagery across all your social media sites strengthens your brand as an artist. It looks more professional and official. People won't wonder if they are on the correct page if everything matches as opposed to having different themes and pictures on each account.

Try and use the same URL address for each social media site. This increases your searchability as an artist and makes you easier to find. For many social platforms you will need to customise your URL as you are given a random series of characters to start off with, which doesn't appear on search engines.

KEY PROMOTION AROUND AN EVENT

Ways to promote your event before, during and after

Promotion is crucial for the successful running of an event. If promotion isn't carried out effectively, it's unlikely that you will engage with, mobilise and grow your fan base. So targeting certain events you are involved with is key to bringing the energy to highlighting not only you as an artist but the event as well.

Allow a few weeks or months to promote your event, giving enough time for people to make plans and to ensure as many people are aware of the event as possible.

Who to contact

Local media are often cheap and free! Contact your local newspapers and radio stations; they may be able to offer you space to advertise the event. Contact or post on websites or forums. There are lots of listing websites such as Gumtree that you are able to add your event to.

Social media: it's free, it's easy and a lot of people have it. Make an event on your social media platforms and invite everyone, then promote it to make sure it's shared by anyone involved as this will spread the word.

Put up posters and distribute leaflets. Word of mouth is a really effective form of promotion, so tell everyone! Engage with your friends and fans and get them to spread the word about your event.

Just before the event

You could if relevant have signs up around the event and also on routes to the event, that way you give people the opportunity to pop in and see what's going on.

Social media becomes useful again; keep updating your social media throughout the day, as it will attract people who may not have decided to go, or at least remind them. Encourage other acts at your event to also post about the event as their fans may come along too.

During an event

Have posters up including your social media links and/or the next gig date, which ideally will be already organised.

Give out leaflets, either as people come in or at the end, on the tables and bars. The leaflets should include your social media links and/or the next gig date. Always ask the venue and/or promoter if that's ok. Ideally your leaflets will have space for people to add their details too, like a mobile number or email address, for you to contact them about future events.

Promote yourself on stage at the end of your set: mention where they can find you after the performance and/or on the Internet and/or the next local gig. Also invite them to talk to you at the bar or at the end.

Sell or give away merchandise; CDs and T-shirts are the most popular.

Most importantly engage with your audience! If they have taken the time to come and see you, come out after and thank them. Drop into the conversation the next gig you have or get them to follow you on Facebook or Twitter. Quite popular these days, if you have a sizeable crowd, is a selfie with the audience in the background and ask audience members to share or tag themselves in when you post the picture on social media.

After an event

Flyers are a good way of making sure people know what you're doing, even when they're leaving. Doing this yourself or getting someone to hand out flyers to everyone as they leave can help to promote any future events you have.

Follow up the gig by thanking fans on your social media platforms, by emailing them or by text. Use the mailing lists obtained during the event to continue promoting other events you may have to offer.

Getting feedback is a good way of seeing what was good or bad about the event. Ask your fans for feedback and thank them for it and let them know you will bear it in mind for future events.

Upload pictures and videos of your sound check, back stage preparation and performance at the event on your social media sites as a way of showing what exactly happened behind the scenes and what people can expect from future events. Stagger them out, don't release them all at once, and pre-announce that you are releasing the stage pictures from the event. Also get your fans to tag themselves in the pictures so they feel involved in the event. Always remember quality is better than quantity when releasing photos and videos of you.

MERCHANDISE FOR SINGERS

How and what to sell to your fans
Merchandise is great for acts to make extra money at their tours, shows and gigs. It's also a way of promoting yourself and spreading the word through your fans. But what do you sell and how should you sell it?

Which merchandise should you sell?
T-shirts are popular so maybe look to sell T-shirts! Give fans the feeling that they are a part of something and they will love wearing and supporting an act's T-shirt. Make sure when designing your T-shirts that you keep them engaging and interesting so they are desirable. So maybe not just a logo on it; make it a cool T-shirt, so think what people would like to wear anyway. Perhaps have a character or slogan that goes with your brand?

If you want to keep costs down consider having it with fewer colours; having it full colour will be more expensive.

Why not sell them your music on CD or USB? At least that way they can continue to listen to your music. A few other items that are likely to be popular are badges, key rings, posters, pens and stickers. These are good because they cost very little and you can sell them for a small cost.

Synchronise your music merchandise

Use the same display pictures, backgrounds and names! Using the same imagery as across all your social media sites strengthens your brand as an artist. It also looks more professional and official.

Selling merchandise online

Merchandise is a brilliant way of maintaining engagement with your fans, especially those fans that aren't necessarily local to you. Selling merchandise online means that even those fans that can't make it to your shows can still have the opportunity to have merchandise.

Selling merchandise online isn't as hard as it seems, as there are websites whose main purpose is to provide other businesses with a platform to sell their products. An example of this is www.shopify.co.uk, a website where you sign up and then are able to build your store. They take credit card payments, therefore not restricting anyone wishing to buy your merchandise.

Selling merchandise after shows

The most obvious way to sell merchandise is through your shows. You've already got fans there that have paid to come and see you perform, so make sure you take this opportunity to make some money. Fans bring friends, so there's more opportunity to make some money after the show from people who may have not heard you before.

Be disciplined and buy in bulk

Of course be disciplined and don't just spend the money on a night out, as reinvesting the money and buying in bulk what sells could make all the difference. The bigger in bulk you buy the cheaper the unit cost and you can quite easily double your money if you do it correctly.

Selling merchandise could be the difference to making a gig work financially if you sell a few T-shirts and CDs at the event. Of course this can give you the funds to invest further into your act like recording studio time or the next step to develop your music. Bear in mind all the time people will be buying your product thus strengthening your brand.

THE PLATFORMS TO PROMOTE YOURSELF

There are numerous ways of promoting your act nowadays. An online presence is essential, as you want people to be able to easily hear your music! Here are some effective ways of getting your act known to the general public.

Your own website
This is where the traffic from all your social media sites should be directed. It is your main hub of activity. It will be where all news stories, photos, videos etc. will be located. It will also be a place where you can sell merchandise and create mailing lists to keep your fans up-to-date with your goings on via newsletters. Keep all the information organised and keep it updated.

Facebook
Creating a Facebook page is essential for any act these days. It is the central hub of online activity and

social networking. It is where all your photos, gig listings, news etc. should be going first. Application plugins can link it to your main website and all your other social media platforms too.

Twitter

Twitter has many ways of helping promote your act. Using hashtags is a great way to get your act 'trending', which increases your visibility to fans by the keywords you have hash-tagged. You can send tweets to like-minded professionals, who in return can re-tweet you to all their followers. It's a great way of getting widespread exposure and making contacts in the industry.

YouTube

YouTube has helped many unknown singers become household names. Anything can be uploaded on YouTube: music videos, songs without videos, press interviews etc. If you have something recorded, it can be promoted to millions on YouTube.

Local radio

Local radio is a great way of getting your music known to people in your local area. This is where your initial fan base will be located until you can start hitting gigs in other areas of the country. Getting interviews on radio is a great way to spread your news about any new gig dates or EP releases. It will also give you the opportunity to play your music to the listeners. If it all goes well, you could get interviews on there on a frequent basis.

Local press

Giving the local newspapers or magazines your press releases for your new EP or gigs is a good way to get exposure. Universities tend to have student papers as well, so approach these to try and get any interviews or reviews of your gigs and EPs. Making good connections with the local media could lead to larger publications taking notice.

Universities and colleges

Universities and colleges have people who listen to all kinds of music. Students are more likely to go along to gigs for unknown acts if they are local. Head to the student unions to distribute flyers and promote the gigs verbally to the students. Universities tend to have radio stations too, so approaching these would be a good idea to get on their airwaves. Try and get involved in University run events like Fresher's week and balls.

Word of mouth

The more people who you get to your gigs the more likely they will be to talk about you to their friends if you impress them. Put on a good show and engage with your fans and it will only enhance your reputation with them and the likelihood they will bring more friends with them to your next show. Keep the audience happy by interacting with them in person and online as often as you can.

SoundCloud

SoundCloud allows unsigned musicians to share their music across all social media platforms. It can be embedded into your profiles so people can hear your music on your page and share the links on their own.

Music videos

If you shoot a video to accompany your songs it can then be placed on all your social media sites. The more professional and interesting the video the more likely it will be to capture the viewer's imagination. This will increase the amount of comments and shares the video receives. It could prompt interest from the local press and may even spread far and wide across the Internet.

Giving your demo to fans

Handing out your demos at gigs is a good way to get your music heard. Fans love new music, especially when it is free as they are more inclined to give it a listen. They can then pass it on to friends who can get a chance to hear your music.

HOW TO PLAN AN EVENT OR SHOWCASE

Things to do before you put on your event or showcase

Planning a music event can be very time consuming and difficult, especially if you have little contacts and little budget. However, there are always ways to make it happen.

Have objectives

First things first, you've got to know why you want to plan the event. Knowing what you're trying to achieve can help you guide your planning in the right direction. This could be an EP or single release or perhaps support of a local charity or worthy cause.

Choose a venue

The venue is one of the most important aspects of planning a music event. The location and day determines who can and can't make it to an event. If you're on a low budget, a small local venue may be best; some won't charge much at all if they see your event as an opportunity to make money via bar sales.

However your gig is as only as good as the venue you choose, so checking out the sound system and engineer at work ahead of booking a venue can be time well spent. Research all the main local music venues and arrange to go down to see if it matches your aspirations for the event. As always planning is everything!

Selecting a venue that your fan base can easily travel to and park at is vital. So consider the nearest bus and rail links. There's no point picking a venue that your fans can't get to very easily.

Considerations when booking a venue

Location - it's always going to be best to have a venue easy to find and easily accessible. Capacity - if it's too big the event could look empty and lack atmosphere. If it's too small it may not be able to accommodate all those wanting to attend the event; although it can create a good buzz if you sell out quickly and not everyone who wants to attend can. Cost is again vital as there is no point having the best event ever but potentially losing a lot of money. Finally ease of communication with the venue and its availability - are the staff at the venue helpful and easy to deal with?

Support artists

It's sensible to also have other acts perform too. There are a few reasons to have more than one act play; it gives potential to increase your audience numbers, thus revenue, whilst also giving you a chance to widen your own fan base.

It's also important to pick other acts that will bring a fan base and promote the event too! It's a missed opportunity to have 3 or 4 support acts that are brilliant but aren't prepared to promote the event and bring fans, because you will just end up with the same numbers as if you were playing a gig on your own.

Go and see other local artists perform at their own gigs; watch if they promote it well and are they well attended. Better still; see if you can play at their gig too.

Once you've decided who would be great support, you will need to decide a ticket split with them or an agreement that they are motivated to promote and sell the gig to their fans.

Choose similar artists

We all have genres of music we prefer to listen to and some we try to avoid. For a music event, especially if on a small scale, it's best to stick with the same genre throughout so that the audience are more likely to stay for the whole event rather than just one act. The planning and promotion of the event should aim to reflect this, thus becoming more appealing and likely to interest general music lovers.

Choosing a date

The date and day of the week can be a decision maker on whether people attend your event or not. It's wise to look at a date far into the future, that way you have time to plan and promote your event.

When deciding a date, do a quick search on other events on that date in your chosen area and avoid perhaps big shows, local festivals and events at your school, college or university if you are studying, so do the planning. There's no point planning your event if a large proportion of your potential audience may be going elsewhere on that day! It's also more likely that venues will have less availability at weekends so planning early is always the best way.

Promote your event

Using social media to promote your event, you just have to ensure that you have enough people who care about the event to share it across their profiles and invite other people. 'Word of mouth' can be a great way to advertise and social networks make that very easy! You can also use local websites or newspapers to list events and get radios to advertise too. Try and get local media involved in the event if it's for a worthy cause or charity.

Posters and leaflets can now be produced cheaply and are effective and professional in promoting events.

Ticket selling

Although selling tickets in advance is more work than selling them on the door, it does mean once someone has bought a ticket they are committed to the event. Ensure you get all the support acts selling tickets too. Even something as simple as a rainy day can sometimes lead to potential gig goers deciding to stay in for the evening rather than coming to your event. If their ticket is already paid for then they are more likely to attend.

Twelve
RELEASING AND SELLING MUSIC

HOW TO DISTRIBUTE YOUR MUSIC

It's more important than ever for singers to take the do-it-yourself approach when it comes to promoting and selling music. With fewer record labels signing artists it's crucial for singers to adopt that hands-on attitude.

When a fan base is built up and your songs are perfected you will want to get your music out there, not just for the fans to hear and generate more interest but also hopefully to make some income; so how do you distribute your music?

What format is best?
There are two forms of distributing and sharing your music: physical and digital sales.

Previously the main way to distribute your music was through physical formats, which meant making CDs and having them distributed into record shops and selling them at gigs. It's however quite common for some label releases to not even manufacture a physical product. Certainly for the individual, CDs are great for selling at gigs and events to generate income and used as a marketing tool for people to take from the event.

Creating physical products such as CDs is a time consuming process that also includes higher costs due to manufacture, artwork, printing etc. This can tie your money up until they are sold. Digital sales allow you to sell directly to fans and after setting up your account you will have no further costs and you can upload an unlimited amount of tracks.

On the flipside some would advocate giving a physical product such as CDs away for free at each gig you perform at, thus reaching out to a much wider audience than just those that want to buy a copy. With CD manufacture possible for very little cost per CD, it is a consideration for a bigger goal in winning over the loyalty of the fans. Perhaps the middle ground would be to give away an EP or live sampler but sell the album.

Distributing music online

To distribute your music to online retailers such as iTunes or Amazon MP3 you can consider using what's called an 'aggregator'. An aggregator puts your music up for sale on all the top online retailers at the same time. Dealing with the online retailers individually can be extremely time consuming and complex, so save yourself the hassle and use an aggregator.

Be warned: although using an aggregator is advantageous for getting your music distributed online, it however doesn't mean that all the hard work is done for you. Don't expect people to just stumble across your music online. You will still need to work hard to promote your music; otherwise your tracks will sit there untouched, generate little or no sales and be a waste of your time.

Aggregator, not alligator!

The main thing to remember is without fans it will be near impossible to raise funds independently. Selling music online relies on the artist's willingness to work hard and promote their act in order to build a loyal fan base that will be excited by the notion that you'll be selling your music online.

Aggregators

With aggregators your music gets distributed, with the ability to get your music chart eligible, to a wide variety of online retailers, for which you keep all royalties and the rights to the music.

There is generally an initial one-off payment to be made for every single/EP/album you upload. The prices vary depending on which services you choose and services can require a small monthly subscription fee for their services.

In general it takes 2-3 weeks before your music will be on all the sites and you will be paid monthly. According to who you go with you can receive daily and weekly sales reports to see how each release is selling and in general it is a month-by-month contract so you can cancel at any time.

Make sure your release is chart eligible

Avoid using more than one aggregator site when selling your music online. There is no need, and using different aggregators will result in your track having multiple barcode numbers, resulting in two versions of the same content and confusion.

The other thing to take note of is that if you have aspirations on making the charts, whether nationally or specialist charts like the Indie chart, you will need to ensure that they are registered as being chart eligible. Also, at the time of writing this, streaming and the amount of times your song is downloaded and listened to will also count towards a chart position.

RELEASING YOUR MUSIC IN THE UK

Releasing your music can be easier than you think. However planning and timing is everything. Make sure you give your release every chance to succeed.

Make sure the timing is right; it's pointless releasing your music until you have some sort of fan base built up, with a fan base interest and backing to give it an initial push and momentum. Otherwise your investment may struggle to bear any fruit by selling very little copies of your music or not getting any sought after promotion.

Register your music
As a singer you want to make money out of your music, so make sure you register your songs to PRS (Performing Rights Society). Registering with them makes sure the songwriter and publisher receive their royalties for every play it gets. Of course as mentioned earlier in the book a publisher can collect this on your behalf too for a cut of the income.

Get your artwork sorted
You want your fans to recognise your artwork when they look for music. This artwork is likely to be the thumbnail people click on to purchase your music so make sure it's something you're confident with. It's also important that your artwork is consistent with you and instantly recognisable, in sync with your act's image on stage, across all your social media platforms and promotion.

Make your music available online
It sounds obvious, but making your music available online is essential as iTunes and Amazon at the time of going to print are becoming the most used platforms for fans buying music. You could lose out on sales if you fail to distribute your music on the majority of the popular websites. An aggregator is also a great way to ensure your release is available across a multitude of platforms.

Get on YouTube
YouTube is the most popular place for people to search for videos, so it makes sense that your music

can be found on there. If people are considering buying your album or your songs then they're likely to want to get a sample of what you sound like. YouTube is the perfect place for this. Again involve your fan base to gain initial interest.

Decide on a release date

To build up the excitement of your music release it's best to set a date a couple of months before. Setting a date for release also allows you to create a buzz within your fan base that can be maintained throughout the countdown to your release. Some online platforms will allow you to do pre-sales as well so always strongly consider doing that.

Build up media attention

As your release date gets closer it's important you start building up the media attention your music has got. This is when you need to approach radio and media to see if they are willing to give you a slot or a plug to promote your music release.

As an act you're a small business trying to get more attention, so make sure you have set budgets and targets to reach so you know you've achieved what you wanted to. If budget dictates you could look to employ the services of a PR company.

Radio plugger

As always take things to a level yourself but if it's too much for you to do everything, the timing is right and funds allow, then consider a radio plugger. Again doing your research is essential and quite often it will be the case that the better pluggers will only consider music from PR companies, labels or management.

It is likely you will need a large budget to employ the services of a plugger, with no guarantee of results. So consider very carefully.

HOW TO PROMOTE YOUR MUSIC

This section is going to very much repeat and reiterate the disciplines we've previously gone through; however, they are just essential, so you're going to have it again in summary. Promoting your music is essential for the success of your act. If you aren't promoting your own music, no one else is going to. By promoting your music you build up a fan base that can spread the word even further.

Social media
It's the most obvious way and not very original, but it's popular for a reason. With YouTube and SoundCloud being the strongest contenders for artists to promote their music, you'd be missing out a huge opportunity not to have an account.

Getting your social media engagement and content right is vital. For example on Facebook if you post too little you are in danger of getting lost in people's news feeds and forgotten. Post too much however and you will irritate your fans! Striking the right balance is essential in keeping your current fans engaged and growing your fan base.

Gig as much as you can
You need people to hear your music and have the opportunity to see you perform live as well; this is where gigging comes in. Having gigging experience

not only helps to promote your music and you as a singer, but it also gives you real life experience of performing on stage and in front of an audience. This experience will help you to develop and improve for future gigs, as you will be able to find out which songs work, what your fan base is like and whether your crowd is enjoying your music. Perhaps start with smaller gigs and open mic nights before embarking on larger gigs.

Working hard promoting the gig, promoting yourself at the gig and promoting yourself after will all assist in advancing your brand and music.

Give stuff away
You should always have leaflets to hand out at your gigs, but of course everyone loves a freebie too, so if you've got a big enough fan base then why not give them something to remember you with.

After you've played at a gig, give some badges or demo CDs away; that way your fans receive something and are more likely to listen to you again. Make sure the CD is professionally recorded and represents you in the best way possible; quality rather than quantity is key. Running competitions through your social media is also an idea, giving away freebies to interact with your fans and keep them engaged.

MUSIC SYNCHRONISATION

Have you ever wondered how that theme tune to your favourite TV show ever made it to where it was?

It could have been written specifically for the show or it could have been part of artist being signed to a music synchronisation deal.

A music synchronisation deal involves granting a licence with an agreement with the copyright holder of a composition allowing the licensee to "sync" music with some kind of visual media output.

Sync deals can apply to various media including TV programmes, documentaries or series, films and trailers, YouTube Clips, business presentations, advertising and video games to name the main ones.

Music synchronisation
When an audio/visual project producer wants to use a recording in their work, they must contact and gain agreement with both the owner of the sound recording (the record label if signed), and the owner of the composition (songwriter or via publishing company if signed).

Make sure your tracks are up to scratch
It sounds obvious but when a producer wants a piece of music to accompany his project whether it's a film, advertisement or television show, it needs to be of perfect recording quality.

Record two versions of everything
Whilst a producer may want a light hearted ballad for his romantic comedy's end credits, often an instrumental track is all that's needed, so ensure you record a separate version of your songs without vocals. You could perhaps consider some extra compositional layers to thicken up the sound. This

could be the difference between getting a music synchronisation deal or not.

How to submit a track for music synchronisation

Getting a music synchronisation deal is no easy task as generally there is a lot of competition. There are multiple ways you can get involved in synchronisation deals but mainly they are forwarded via publishers, managers, digital distributors and aggregators.

U.C.B.
LIBRARY

Lightning Source UK Ltd.
Milton Keynes UK
UKOW06f1243140817
.307195UK00008B/142/P